Over the past decade the publishing industry has undergone dramatic changes. The old, proud publishing houses have, for the most part, become virtually indistinguishable from other commercial establishments, delegating their traditional editorial functions to agents whose primary purpose is to meet the demands of the market. Increasingly, authors are eschewing the agent-to-publisher-to-mass market route and are turning to on-demand, self- publishing. Whether the process includes a traditional publisher or not, editorial niceties and fact-checking often have no place in the process.

This has led to a number of problems, the worst of which is – from the Academy's point of view –the great increase in "junk science" being published both as fiction and non-fiction. The Academy therefore offers those Academy members who have written a science-heavy book, the opportunity to submit the book to our editors for review *of the science therein.* The manuscript receives the same rigorous scientific review that we accord articles published in our Journal. If the reviewer(s) determine(s) that the science is accurate, the author may then continue the publishing process of choice and the book may display the seal of The Washington Academy of Sciences. In cases where the Academy editors determine that the book is scientifically accurate but requires editing, they may return the manuscript to the author and request that it be satisfactorily edited.

To Susie –
I'll miss you.
Peg

ISBN: 0615790631
ISBN 13: 9780615790633

Library of Congress Control Number: 2013936625
Washington Academy of Sciences
Washington DC

ACKNOWLEDGMENTS

In order to get it right, novelists need a lot of help. And we had the best help around. We are greatly indebted to Astronomer Bill Hartkopf who gave us a terrific private tour of the U.S.Naval Observatory. If your visit to Washington D.C. should coincide with one of the Observatory's Open Houses, don't miss it. The library alone is stunning even without the dome.

Engineer and amateur astronomer Joe Morris prevented us from making a bushel basket full of engineering errors. We quickly learned not to leave dome without him.

And for us city dwellers, we couldn't have done without the help of John Kinnard and the town of Thurmont, located near Camp David in the Catoctin Mountains. They showed us what a small town should be like. Our town of Bella Villa is purely fictional, but the help of John and Thurmont went a long way toward making Bella Villa believable. The other town in the book, unlike Bella Villa, is a discouraged mess. Which caused us to wonder why some towns survive recessions and others go belly-up. Conclusion was that the lucky towns have leaders who meet adversity and kick it in the teeth.

Mary and Barry Jackson Clark, of Peaceful Hollow Farm in Westminster, Maryland gave us an alpaca education. If there is an animal cuter than an alpaca, we don't know of one – and we've met lots of kittens. The herd's guardian llamas are both stately and endearing. We wish we could manage that.

Our mentor, Kathryn Johnson of Write by You, as always, steered us in the right direction when we wandered off.

A special salute to Sue Fisher, our advisor on all things military.

And finally, thanks to our redactor, editor, and friend, Molly Cameron – who took time off from her busy schedule to tell us what great writers we are. Now *that's* a friend.

NOTE: Glossaries of Yiddish-English and Australian
Slang-English follow the Epilogue

THE CASE OF THE ECLIPSED ASTRONOMER

a bea goode mystery

Peg Kay
with Dr. Sethanne Howard

Washington Academy of Sciences

Prologue

October 1991

An office in New South Wales, Australia at the headquarters of the
Australia Telescope National Facility

Larry Pottle was a satisfied man. Here he sat, a staff astronomer in
what was the newest, fastest, glitziest radio telescope array in the world
and he was going to the States to talk about it. He leaned back and
stretched, just as the mail arrived in the hands of the luscious Maggie.
"Package for you, Sweetie". She dropped the package on his desk.
Larry admired her departure.

"Well, stone the crows," he muttered as he looked at the return
address. From Uncle Morgan, recently deceased, of the Army
Observatory near Washington, D.C. "The old guy must have posted this
just before he carked it."

Larry opened the package and discovered that he was the recipient
of the old recluse's research notes. He thumbed through them, then
reached for the latest edition of the *Astronomical Journal*, finding his
way to a well-worn page. "Holy dooly!" He picked up all of the
material and high-tailed to the director's office, made a cursory knock
on the door and barged in.

Ham looked up. "Nice to see you, mate."

"Take a look at this, Ham." Larry plunked the stuff on Ham's desk.

1

Ham did a quick look. "Cripes! Whaddya think we should do about it?"

"I'm going to be in D.C. for the Conference. Can you extend my stay for a day? Letitia Krackov is at the Army Observatory. Might be a good idea to talk to her before we do anything."

"No sooner approved than done." Ham reached for the phone.

Chapter 1

October 7, 1991

"Alex! Put your hand where it belongs."

Alex, aggrieved. "This *is* where it belongs."

I shot a glance at my tousled-haired husband, sitting innocently in the passenger seat beside me. "You loon, you're going to get us into an accident."

"Oh, awright."

I shot a second glance. He was now sitting with hands folded in his lap, looking adorably angelic, and whistling "I'm Called Little Buttercup."

Alex and I both worked at the Laboratory for Industrial Technology (LIT), I as a management scientist reporting to the Deputy Director, Alex as a computer scientist and senior technical guy. LIT itself was part of a larger entity, the Department of Trade and Industry (DoTI, pronounced "dotty"). I was shortly to get an inkling of just how dotty the Department was.

I pulled into a space in the LIT parking lot and turned off the motor. Alex leaned over and gave me a serious kiss.

"Howsabout a snoggle, keed?"

"Don't mind if I do." We were in the midst of the snoggle when there came a rapping on our windowpane. We sprang apart.

It was Don Cromarty, my boss. "If you get to the part where you're making babies, I'm selling tickets."

We got out of the car and joined Don.

Alex glared at him. "I'm glad to see you, too."

Don laughed and Alex trotted off toward his lab. I caught up with him, grabbed his ears, kissed him on the nose, and returned to Don. We walked toward the admin wing.

"D'ja read the paper this morning?"

I nodded. "You mean the Anita Hill-Clarence Thomas brouhaha?"

"Yeah. Just in time for his hearings as Supreme Court Justice. Do you think he really sexually harassed her?"

"Hard to tell how it'll play out," I said. "I can't think of any reason why she would have accused him if it wasn't true. The woman is a law professor at a major university. Starting this kind of a stink is not going to make life on campus particularly pleasant."

We parted at the entrance, Don to his office, me to mine.

Walking, I pondered my life. Husband I adored. Couldn't ask for a better job or boss. And a LIT Director whom I had known and loved for years. Darn close to perfection.

I'm uncomfortable sitting behind a desk while talking to whomever drops into my office. So my desk is backed up to the wall opposite the door. When someone comes in, I only have to swivel to be face-to-face, with no barrier between. As I opened my office door, the eminent Dr. P.I. Lee swivelled to greet me. Dr. Lee is the LIT Director and the beloved Uncle Pie. My first (deceased) husband, Harry, and I were the honorary niece and nephew of Uncle Pie and Aunt Bessie.

Pie was born of a Chinese mathematician father and a Jewish housewife mother. Always beautifully tailored, shoes shined, hair brushed, the illusion was shattered by his outrageous Brooklyn accent. He came to LIT from UCLA via MIT at the request (pleading?) of the Secretary of the Department.

"Hi, Pie." I gave him a kiss and plunked myself in the visitor's chair. "What brings you here?"

"Did you see the story in this morning's Post?"

I looked at Pie, puzzled. It was not like him to make idle chit-chat during office hours. "Saw the headline and skimmed the story. It's a stunner."

"Yeah. It is that."

Silence.

I studied Pie. "What is it that you're avoiding telling me?"

"*Bubele*, it's a long story, well, maybe not so long. You know the US Naval Observatory?"

"Uh huh. In the District, near the Vice President's house."

"Ever been there?"

"No. Pie, you don't want me to take some visiting dignitaries on a tour of USNO, do you?"

"No, no, nothing like that. It's like this. USNO has been there forever and a few years ago, the Army noticed it and decided that if the Navy had an observatory, the Army should have an observatory."

"You're kidding."

"I wish I were. Anyway, the Army found some pocket change and built an observatory about fifteen miles from here on Blessing Mountain near Bella Villa County."

"Blessing Mountain isn't a mountain, it's a big hill. You can't do serious astronomical work there. That's goofy!"

"*So nu?* It's not the only goofy thing the Army's ever done. Anyway, now they agree with you and they're trying to get rid of the thing."

"And?"

"And DoTI wants to acquire it."

"What in God's name for?"

"Well, the official reason is that the facility is capable enough to examine near-Earth asteroids to see if they can be mined for metals useful in industry. A speculation that may be true. There are almost nine thousand asteroids with diameters over forty-five meters. They think (the Secretary didn't tell me who 'they' are) that some of those asteroids have high levels of platinum. If so, one of those asteroids could contain the equivalent amount of platinum mined in a whole year on Earth. That would make each small asteroid worth several billion dollars."

"That's very impressive. Now tell me what's the unofficial reason?"

"I dunno if there is one. But the Secretary's kid – he's about twelve – is an astronomy nut. I think the Secretary wants him to have a telescope."

I digested this. "Okay. Now that we're both on the same side of the Looking Glass – why are you telling me this?"

"Because we want you to spend a couple of weeks there, sizing up the place and evaluating the personnel. Make recommendations about whom we want to keep."

"Pie, no! I love it here. Alex and I take turns driving to work every day. We only have one car. Don will have a cow. Won't you miss me?"

"I'll miss you. If anything happens on the Hill I'll probably screw it up. But the Secretary asked for you. I argued but the *shmegegge* thinks he's doing you a favor – a reward for nearly getting yourself killed the last time you helped DoTI out. He says it's a good career move for you; he's probably right.

"You can keep driving with Alex. I'll get you a government car to go from here to there. It's not much out of the way."

"Rats! When do I start?"

"Tomorrow morning. They'll have a briefing book over here in an hour or so. I'll round up a car for you. I'll call and let them know that you're coming."

"I bet they'll be just thrilled. Have you told Don?"

"Not yet. Would you like to tell him?"

I scowled at Pie.

"Okay, okay," he said, "I'll tell him. Are you going to eat lunch in the cafeteria?"

I nodded.

"I'll bring you the book there. Noon?"

"That'll be good."

Pie departed.

So much for the perfect life.

A long-winded Congressional staffer called me about 11:45, so I was a few minutes late getting to the cafeteria. I picked up my grilled cheese and looked around for Alex, spotted him sitting with Don and Pie at a table for four, and joined them.

"I take it that Pie has told you about my exile?"

Don took a bite of his sub, talked around the salami. "Yeah, no more canoodling at lunchtime for a while."

"You won't think it's so darn funny when *you* have to show visiting firemen around."

Pie handed me a thin notebook. "Here's your homework."

"Thanks. I think."

I glanced through the book, managing not to spill more than a few crumbs and a dollop of cheese on it. I set it down.

Pie turned to me. "Did you see the work description in the briefing book?"

"Yep. I understand what they're doing, but I can't figure out why they're doing it?"

"What *are* they doing?" Don asked.

Pie answered, "The facility's sole astronomer is taking pictures with a CCD camera attached to the telescope. The two-dimensional images are part of a survey of galaxies. USAO is surveying relatively nearby elliptical galaxies to get their light curves. I talked to an astronomer friend who thinks it's moderately useful, but not worth the upkeep of a whole observatory. It doesn't make sense. To me, anyway."

"Why aren't they doing more?" Alex asked.

"Well," said Pie, "I don't think..."

A young woman with a loaded tray approached.

"Hi, Becky. I know we've only got a little piece of the action, but are you finding the genetic research challenging?"

"Hi, Dr. Pie. Very. At my level, I'm probably getting more to do here than if I were at the National Institutes of Health competing for projects with the big boys. It's only..." She trailed off.

"Only what, Beck?"

"Sometimes I wonder about the ethics of some of this stuff."

"Understandable. So do I. Let's you and Don and I have lunch tomorrow and talk about it. Are both of you free?"

"I'm in," said Don.

"Sure," said Becky.

"Can I join you?" said Alex.

"Absolutely," said Pie.

And I'm going to be trapped on top of a dumb hill, thought I.

"Where was I?" Pie asked.

Alex answered, "You were about to explain why USAO wasn't doing more than taking pictures of nearby galaxies."

"Oh, yeah. Their facility isn't capable of doing much more. The limitations are a combination of the environment and the instrument. Here, actually all along the East Coast, the interference by city lights limits the vision to just the brightest celestial objects plus the fact that USAO has a 36" telescope — barely research grade. The bigger telescopes are 4 meters and are put on the top of real mountains in less populated areas near the West Coast. Nowhere on the East Coast is feasible. Only radio telescopes can operate around here and even they need a 'quiet zone'."

Pie looked at his watch. "I'd better get going. Lenore has a hissy fit if I'm late for a meeting."

Ben, who was just arriving, greeted Pie as he was leaving. Ben grabbed his seat.

Don said, "With all the stuff Pie has to do, I don't know where he finds the time to learn about astronomy."

"Easy," said Ben. "He just buys a book and puts it under his pillow. He learns in his sleep."

Don, who should have known better, asked, "How does he do that?"

Ben smiled charmingly. "Cosmosis."

Chapter 2

October 8, 1991

I had a brief meeting with Don and Pie and let my troops know that if they needed me for anything they could call me at the Observatory. My troops, who number five and a half souls, are responsible for most of the junk that befalls Federal employees. We are not organized in the traditional Federal Way. The Office of Personnel Management has titles, for instance Economist, and the job description that goes with the title. However, once the title becomes a person, the person and the agency can agree on any set of duties desired. I, for instance, am classified as an economist. If I am an economist, Mother Teresa drives the Indy 500. I have a doctorate in Management Science.

Pie, Don, and I form LIT's senior management team. There were a few other senior managers when Pie took over the agency, but he was of the quite sensible opinion that if the technical people knew their jobs they didn't need a helluva lot of management. Alex and his counterpart on the biology side of the house convinced him that the techies knew what they were doing. So, as the occasions arose, Pie rid the agency of the managerial bloat. He kept me to handle high-level junk such as dealing with the myriad predators (e.g. Congress) who had designs on our budget. Don handles the spillover from Pie's desk and attends meetings that demand an SESer to be in attendance. Don also makes sure that we are apprised of the fortunes of the Little League teams that he coaches.

I have a small staff of my own.

Jim Daley handles the routine nonsense generated by the Congress and requests from school groups for tours or speakers. He's a lanky tow-headed guy with a bizarre sense of humor. He has been known to greet school groups while wearing an Albert Einstein rubber mask and talking with what he claims is a German accent. He sounds more like the Swedish chef. The school teachers and their wards love him.

Jeanne Cameron handles travel, oversees the support staff, and takes care of non-sensitive personnel matters. Aside from Pie, she is the only person in the admin wing who is consistently tactful and unflappable. Which is why she provides a buffer between Ben and the typing pool.

Half of Ben – the half that analyzes trade statistics – reports to me. The other half – the half that includes budget – reports to Don. Ben is unique. When our former exec officer went on to other things, we slid Ben into his slot. His sartorial choices run to polyester suits in previously-unrecognized hues and, to top them off, cartoon character ties. He seems to have an inexhaustible supply of ties. My favorite is Wile E. Coyote, but Elmer Fudd is a close runner-up. Normally a sweet-tempered man, when it comes to dealing with typists he morphs into a micromanaging monster. Therefore, he is allowed to deal with typists only through the equable Jeanne.

Marge Dunn, a carrot-topped stunner, takes care of publications of which we have quite a lot. Marge is everything an editor should be. Not only does she know her onions, she knows how to deal with scientists. She is fiercely protective of the integrity of their papers. Other places, both private sector companies and Federal agencies, keep trying to steal Marge, offering riches beyond imagination. But Marge stays – she doesn't need money (her husband cashed out of the dot.com business at its peak) and she loves her job and her colleagues. I know just how she feels.

And then there is Ethel. Ethel had recently been assigned to help Marge with the publications. This has not worked out wonderfully well. But aside from Ethel the Useless, it's a great staff. We work well together and we like one another.

I picked up the government car. It was white, uncomfortable, decrepit, lacking a radio, and mine for the duration. I was almost tempted to decline that junker in favor of my car, which is a spiffy black Mustang convertible. I bought it in 1987, the first year that Ford made convertibles after a long hiatus. When Alex and I married, we decided to get rid of Alex's jalopy and to keep the Mustang. We both love it. However, if I declined the government junker, that would leave Alex without a car should he need it while at LIT. So I made a face at the junker, got in, turned on the motor, and left the lot.

It wasn't long before I reached the two-lane road that climbed through the countryside to Bella Villa County. It was a beautiful drive, but slow. In addition to the sharp bends, occasional farm vehicles pulled out of nowhere and led me at a crawl for a mile or so before turning off. But no mind, the country was gorgeous. The farms mostly contained dairy cows with a leavening of Black Angus. I passed one farm with a herd of thirty or forty odd-looking cows lolling about in the pasture. At least I thought they were cows before I realized that someone was raising alpacas. Why do people raise alpacas?

Aside from the livestock, the route held other charms. Now, at the beginning of October, the leaves were just beginning to turn to their fall colors. There was just a tinge of red and yellow on the maples. In a couple of weeks it would be spectacular.

There was also a sprinkling of little towns – pockets containing a gas station, a post office, a bank, and a main street with a general store, a café, and – in the larger of them – a hardware store and a ladies' fashion emporium. Right out of a Norman Rockwell magazine cover.

I came to a scenic overlook and paused in my journey. I looked over a landscape of farms and orchards. It was a long way down. Pulling out of the overlook I noticed that the right shoulder barrier had been smashed and temporarily patched with yellow tape. A vase holding flowers sat next to it. I shuddered. It was a *very* long way down.

Inevitably, I reached the Observatory. There were a couple of little outbuildings, one of them no more than a shed. The main building was odd looking. There was a one-story, semi-circular structure connected by a wide enclosed corridor to a taller edifice that contained the dome. Trip-hammers sounded from behind the dome.

I parked the car in one of the slots between a bright red pickup and a BMW. The BMW had its own assigned space. Colonel Ambrose Burnside. The car sported an American flag bumper sticker. One of the legion of bumper sticker patriots driving foreign cars.

I walked to the door of the one-story building and entered. A bell rang, summoning a very attractive young woman.

"Hi, I'm Lorelei Loofus, known mostly as Lorrie." She held out her hand.

I shook it. "I'm Bea Goode." I got the look I always get when I tell people my name. I use my maiden name professionally, so that people who don't know me well but want to find me can do so. Despite that, I would have taken Alex's name, but "Bea Carfil" isn't any better than "Bea Goode."

"Colonel Burnside is waiting for you." She turned to take me to her leader.

"Is he a full colonel? The briefing book said he's a lieutenant colonel."

"He told us to call him "colonel".

Uh oh. One of those.

She led me across a very large room containing a refectory table and chairs. Lining the room were offices and a larger room that was probably used for staff meetings. We arrived at a heavy door that opened onto the connecting corridor. The corridor contained a men's room adjacent to an office. Loofus opened the office door and stood aside. A uniformed, portly, flush-faced man stood behind a large desk.

The desk was notable for the absence of so much as a paper clip on its surface.

"That will be all, Mrs. Loofus," he said.

She closed the door behind her.

The man turned his attention to me. "I am Colonel Burnside. Do you wish to be called Mrs. or Miss or, heaven-forfend, Ms. Goode?" He smiled a thin-lipped smile.

Already I was not overly fond of this bozo. "I wish to be called Dr. Goode, Lieutenant Colonel."

He scowled. "It is now 10:30 ack emma. I expect you to be here at 9:00 ack emma in the future."

Uninvited, I sat down in one of the plush visitors' chairs and smiled. "We don't always get what we expect, do we?"

He sat down, his hands hidden behind the desk.

"Well, what is it you think we can do for you?"

"Aside from a tour of the physical plant, I would like to interview each of your staff privately."

"I am afraid that will be impossible. I will attend each interview."

I stood up. "Lieutenant Colonel, I am here to facilitate the transfer of this facility [did I really say that?] to the Department of Trade and Industry. I am an experienced management scientist and I know the best way to do this. Your alternatives are: you permit me to do my job as I see fit or I leave now and tell the Secretary that you refuse to cooperate. Now which is it?"

His flush grew deeper. "I will permit you to interview the staff. But

I will also call your immediate superior and report your insolence."

"Thank you for the permission. Would you like Mr. Cromarty's or Dr. Lee's phone number?"

"That will be all, Ms. Goode."

A young guy emerged from the men's room as I departed the military lair. He courteously opened the heavy door for me. As soon as it closed behind us, he grinned and said, "Way to go, Dr. Goode!"

I stared at him. "Do you have a listening post in the men's john?"

"Yep, when Call-me-Colonel took over here he had his office and the john carved out of the corridor, and the wall between the two rooms is just a sheet of drywall."

"But can't he hear you, too?"

"Only when we flush. We're careful not to talk in there so he doesn't know we can hear him." He stuck out his hand. "I'm Bobby Figgle."

I shook it. "I'm Bea."

He nodded. "Lorrie told us."

The office doors surrounding the common room began to open and people to emerge. Bobby got a faraway look in his eyes. A muted chorus of groans ensued.

Bobby jumped up on the refectory table, raised his hand for silence, and chanted,

There once was a woman named Bea,

Came to see just what she could see,

And what did she find?

The milit'ry mind,

And thought what a crumb bum is he.

I applauded.

"Please, don't encourage him," said someone with a slight Australian accent.

"Does he do that often?" I asked.

"Yeah," a big, rugged-looking man answered. "It's like T-T-Tourette's Syndrome, only with limericks. I'm Chuck Hadaman."

"You run the machine shop?"

He nodded.

I turned to the Australian accent. "The briefing book says you're Worley Doolittle. Is that right?"

Another nod.

There was one more man. This one with a pathetic comb-over and a slight paunch. He was drinking from a coffee cup. "And you are?"

He jumped, spilling coffee over his jacket. Unnoticeable among the other stains. "Oh, thit!" he said. Then, "I'm Tristram Gomping."

"Is Dr. Krackov here?"

Doolittle shook his head. "The Pulsar Meeting is going on in D.C. today. She'll be back tomorrow."

"I hope you didn't stay here on my behalf."

He shook his head. "Naw. I'm not interested in pulsars. There's a meeting on deep survey maps later this month and I'll go to that one. We'll have Bad Movie Night then, too."

Bad Movie Night. Right. I'll find out later.

"Is your exec officer – George Wumpus – here?"

The texture of the air deadened.

"You don't know?" asked Bobby.

"Know what?"

Bobby turned to Hadaman. "You tell her, Chuck."

"G-g-gee," Hadaman began, "This was so bizarre that I thought even the D.C. papers would have picked it up."

"The front pages of the Washington papers are full of Anita Hill and Clarence Thomas. Please continue."

"Well, there's a pumpkin cannon on one of the local farms..."

"A what?"

"It's the local October to December sport around here. They fabricate a long tube and hook it to a compressed air pump. People pay about a buck a shot to have it loaded with a p-p-pumpkin and they aim at a target about a football field away. The pumpkin leaves the cannon at about about eighty miles an hour.

"So yesterday morning the guy who runs the pumpkin shoot goes to open up, discovers that the compressor is running, and goes out into the f-f-field to see what's up. He finds George's body. He was covered in smashed pumpkin."

Loofus added, "Call-me-Colonel alerted us yesterday afternoon. I suppose he didn't think you had a need to know. We're having a memorial service tonight at the Presbyterian Church in Bella Villa."

"Does anyone know what happened?"

Shrugs all around.

For a minute I was speechless while this sunk in.

This was clearly not an accident. So someone deliberately murdered the exec officer. But was he murdered because he was the exec officer? In which case I had just signed on to spend a couple of weeks with a killer. Or was he murdered because he was him? There didn't seem to be any indication one way or another. Oh boy.

"Well, we'd better get to work. I'd appreciate it if someone gave me a tour of the place and then I'd like to interview each of you."

Doolittle raised his hand. "I'll take you on the tour. While we're gone, Bobby can tell the rest of the staff how your interview with Call-me-Colonel went."

I started to shed my coat but Doolittle advised me to keep it on. "The tour will be chilly." I followed him through the heavy door and into the corridor. As we approached another heavy door at the far end of the corridor, the sound of the trip-hammer grew louder. Doolittle explained that the catwalk surrounding the dome was being repaired. He opened the door and we stepped through into darkness.

"Hold it a minute," he said, "while I open the slit."

I could make him out dimly, as he walked across the room. He found a flashlight and pointed it at a white control box. He opened the box and pushed a button. Overhead, two panels parted and light flooded in.

Doolittle returned. "There's a staircase behind you that leads to another door, which opens onto the catwalk. I won't take you up there because it'll be dangerous until repairs are done. We're in the room where the telescope lives." He pointed at the telescope which, in turn, pointed at the slit.

"Over there is the control box, where you control what the dome does. It keeps an electronic log that records those housekeeping functions. That log is transmitted over our network to a backup tape in the shed. The tapes are kept for a week and then we write over them. That little office over there is where I handle observatory matters when I'm not actually observing. It has a heavy door to this room and a normal door to the outside.

"You may have noticed that this room is a bit chilly. That's because the telescope requires ambient temperature. The heavy doors make sure the temperature *stays* at the ambient level."

I examined the telescope. "I expected the telescope to be bigger."

Doolittle laughed. "That's because you've been brainwashed by the Navy. The telescope they have at the Naval Observatory is a monster. It sits in the bedrock under the building. When you want to look through it, you come through the heavy door onto a huge, circular floor with a hole in the middle where the telescope comes through. When you want to use the telescope, the whole floor descends or rises until the end of the telescope is easy to reach. I heard that it's the largest elevator in the world – or at least around here."

"So the telescope is more powerful than the one *you've* got?"

"No, no, no. Bigger ain't better. The one at USNO is a refracting telescope. Those work like a magnifying glass – they use a glass lens to bend the light and bring it into focus. The suckers may have their advantages but they have two big problems – one is that the size of the lens is limited by its own weight and that limits how much you can see, and the other is that the telescope has to be really long and heavy. There also used to be a problem with color distortion – it's a problem with all single lenses. In the early 1800's they corrected for the color distortion by putting two lenses together. The telescope at USNO is one of the last large refracting telescopes made for scientific use. They stopped making them in the early 1890s.

"The one that we have is a reflecting telescope which, by the way, is also anchored in the bedrock. It uses curved mirrors instead of lenses to collect and focus the light so it doesn't have a color distortion problem and the weight of the mirror is not an issue. Also, with a reflecting telescope you can pack a lot more power into a smaller dome.

"Even so, the one we have isn't powerful enough to do heavy astronomical work. The best we can get out of it is to survey nearby elliptical galaxies. So we do do what we can do.

"You got any questions?"

"Just one, for the moment. How do you get the telescope to point where the slit opens?'

"Ah. I let the control box know where I want to look on a given night. Then the control box tells the dome to revolve to the designated place and the slit, which protrudes from the dome, opens and reveals the heavens.

"Any more questions?"

"I'm good for now."

"Okay. Go out the corridor door and I'll follow after I close the slit."

As we walked through the common room, I asked Doolittle about the refectory table.

"Serves two purposes," he said. "Sometimes a couple of us bring our lunch and if we feel like having company, we eat at the table. But the main purpose is for Bobby to jump on it and deliver limericks." Deadpanned.

"A noble calling. But assuming it was here before Bobby, what was its original purpose?"

"Call-me-Colonel has delusions of grandeur. He expected to host exceptionally important meetings befitting his station. He tried it a few times but no one ever came unless he promised free food. And even then only a couple of famished souls ever showed up."

We walked out the front door and Doolittle led me to the larger of the two outbuildings. "This is the machine shop — Hadaman's territory." He opened the door. It looked like a machine shop, all right.

"Chuck knows just about everything there is to know about telescopes. If you had gone to the basement of the dome, you'd have seen a room full of the nuts and bolts and gears needed to keep the instrument – and the rest of the building – running. Tristram works for him part-time."

"Tristram works part-time? "

"Yeh. He just gets paid full-time. The guy's the laziest piece of work I've ever seen."

Doolittle showed me to the shed, which had transmission wires running to it. "This temperature-controlled shed is where we keep the magnetic backup tapes. Chuck reads each day's tape and if there is any indication that something isn't going as smoothly as he would like, he checks the instrument. If something is broke he fixes it.

"By the way, the data that are sent from the dome to the tape travel over our local area network which has drops into each of the offices. I think we're about finished with the tour.

"Are you about ready for lunch?"

"I am that. Where's a good place to eat?"

"No, no. You are the good witch, who came to rescue us from Call-me-Colonel. Our treat."

The restaurant, The Four Leaf Clover, was quite good. Lorrie ordered the lunch special, she-crab soup and Caesar salad, and I followed suit. As did everyone else until it was Tristram's turn. He ordered "thrimp" salad and a well-done steak. From the poisonous looks he got from everyone, I surmised that they intended to split the total check. Doolittle was right. Tristram Gomping was a piece of work indeed.

The company was also quite good – except for Tristram, who kept trying to tell me how much he knew about Pie's area of biological expertise. I think the idiot expected me to recommend that Pie take him to LIT as his assistant or advisor. Or something.

Once back at the Observatory, I began the interviews, starting with Worley Doolittle. He was an unremarkable looking man. Medium height. Medium weight. Hair medium brown with the beginning of a male-pattern bald spot. He told me that he had come to the States about twenty years ago to work as an astronomer at one of the big observatories in California. Shortly before he left Australia, his younger brother died of a massive heart attack. He and his brother were extremely close and when he got here, he simply could not concentrate or work to any good effect. Eventually, he was shunted off to USAO where a top-flight astronomer was not needed. He didn't mind. Except for Call-me-Colonel, he liked his job and his colleagues. Well, maybe not Tristram, but he was never around anyway. He could use a little more money, but what the hell.

Lorrie was married to an astrophysicist who taught at the University of Maryland. She was on the tallish side – about four inches higher than my five four. She had started training as a speech therapist but after a few months she decided that she wasn't cut out for that. She was too impatient. She liked her job at USAO, but as soon as they had enough money for a down payment, they were going to buy a house and have kids. She wasn't going out to work again until the kids were school age. I asked her about her colleagues. She responded that, except for Call-me-Colonel and Tristram, she was fond of them. She told me that Tristram had an odd phonemic disorder, called the *fis phenomenon*. He couldn't distinguish between the "sh" sound, and the "th" sound. That was a problem that kids usually outgrew. It was rare to find it in an adult. "But," she added, "I suppose Tristram never grew up."

"What does he do when he's supposed to be working?"

"He hides. His favorite place is the magnetic tape shed. He either snoozes in there or he plays that stupid flute of his."

"Flute?"

"Not a real flute, it's one of those things that primitive people play – looks a little like a recorder."

"Does he play it well?"

Lorrie gave me a caustic look. "I've heard bagpipes that sound better.

"He walks around carrying a tool box so that people will think he's working – like getting everything 'thip thape.'

"Well, I caught him about to take the tool box, with all those magnetic-tipped screwdrivers, into the magnetic tape shed. He could have corrupted every last tape. Even *I* know better than that."

Chuck Hadaman loved what he did and loved where he worked. He managed to put up with his putative assistant. He didn't really need an assistant. He didn't have enough to do as it was. His sister and her husband had a horse farm and he rode horses every chance he got. When he retired, he'd like a horse farm of his own. The red pickup I'd seen in the parking lot was his. He had a small house in the town of Bella Villa and he felt that he was part of the town, which was pretty lively in a rural sort of way. He loved helping with its various events. He always fabricated something in metal for the homecoming float. Last year, he made two football players chasing a pig. The players' arms and legs moved and the pig squealed. He'd been doing this so long that the town made it an official homecoming event. People sent in float ideas, the mayor and city council picked a winner, and Chuck was challenged to convert it to metal. So far, he hadn't been stymied. He lived for the day when he'd have the chance to grind Call-me-Colonel up in the telescope gears. I think he was joking.

Tristram was Tristram. Smoothing his pitiful comb-over he let me know that his colleagues were not his intellectual equals, not nearly. Was I aware that his extra-curricular activity was as the musicologist for the Culture Club.

I envisioned Tristram in drag playing lead guitar next to Boy George and almost managed to stifle a grin.

"Not *that* Culture Club," he said indignantly. "*My* Culture Club is a serious organization that studies cultures from around the world."

"And you are the musicologist."

"Well, just for the local chapter, but yes."

"Are you trained as a musicologist?"

"I am an autodidact."

He looked at me expectantly to see if I'd ask what an autodidact was. I disappointed him.

"Aside from the fact that they aren't your intellectual equals, do you get along with your colleagues?"

"Thure. Except for that worm, George Wumpus."

"The exec officer who was shot by the pumpkin?"

"That's him. Do you know what that worm did to me?

"What?"

"He turned down my travel request to go the international Culture Club conference. I was supposed to give a paper — a paper that would get me the recognition I deserve and a ticket out of this place." Tristram was coming to a boil.

"But why would the USAO fund your travel to a Culture Club conference?"

"Because with all the hard work I put in here, they owe it to me." He stamped his foot.

"Oh, yes, of course," I said and terminated the interview.

The final interview was with Bobby Figgle. He was a nice looking guy. About five ten. Maybe a hundred fifty pounds. Dark red hair cut close. A good humored look about him. "Bobby," I asked, "what on earth are you doing here? I've looked at your curriculum vita and you could have gone anywhere you wanted. And don't tell me you're interested in mapping near-Earth elliptical galaxies."

Bobby laughed. "No ma'am. I wanted to come here because Letitia Krackov is here and she agreed to mentor me. She gives me about two hours a day. The rest of the time I do my own research. Don't snitch. Call-me-Colonel thinks I came here to look at elliptical galaxies." He paused and looked at me consideringly.

"Hey, when you guys take over, you're not going to turf her out, are you?"

"Of course not. Do you like working with her?"

He looked around. "Ears only?"

"Ears only, cross my heart."

And Bobby said,

> The lady once was a dish,
>
> Now old and somewhat churlish,
>
> She can be quite tart
>
> And if you are smart
>
> You won't try to call her Tish

"Now that you've got that out of your system," I said, "how do you like working with her?"

"It's everything I hoped for. She's the best teacher I've ever had and I've had a lot of good ones. My only regret is that I didn't get to her when she was working instead of just writing about it. If I ever become a first-class astronomer, she'll have had a lot to do with it."

"How would you rate your colleagues?"

Bobby thought. "Worley isn't much of an astronomer, but he's a nice guy and he's doing useful work. He's okay here. Chuck is great. He's a fine machinist. I like him a lot. He doesn't socialize much after work. I asked him once if he wanted to have a beer, but he begged off. Intimated that he keeps his workplace separate from his personal life. Lorrie's a sweetheart. And as for Call-me-Colonel and Tristram – one time they both came into the men's john while I was there and let me tell you..."

Bobby got that faraway look in his eyes.

Uh oh.

There once were two fellas, by chance,

Unable to fill out their pants,

They each had a teeny

Miniature weenie,

Easy to miss at a glance.

The man is incorrigible.

I got my coat and entered the government junker, pointing it back toward LIT. USAO was peopled by an ill-assorted group. Most of them extremely likable, the exceptions being Burnside and Gomping. Burnside will not be DoTI's problem. The military can deal with the bozo. Gomping, however, could be trouble. With a little luck, we can foist him off on the Army also. Doolittle is not actually incompetent; he's good enough for what USAO needs. My ignorance of things astronomical prevents me from judging if he's good enough to study DoTI's asteroids. I'll have to check on that. Hademan appears to be a gem. Too good for USAO? If he's as good as he seems to be, DoTI had better find him more chores or they'll lose him. Lorrie will be fine until she drops her litter. She'll have to be replaced at that time. I'll bet the DoTI human relations department can finger someone suitable who lives up the mountain and would like a transfer closer to home. As for Bobby – he's a post-doc and doesn't belong to us. I wish he did.

I pulled the government junker into the LIT lot and walked over to our car. Alex was leaning on the fender, waiting for me. He embraced me tenderly and said, "Poor babe, I'm sorry you had such a rough time."

I pulled back. "What are you talking about? I think I might even enjoy this assignment."

"That idiot colonel called and complained about you."

"That's the idiot *lieutenant* colonel. Did that bozo really call? Sheesh!"

"Get in the car and I'll tell all." Alex slid into the driver's seat.

Silence while he maneuvered out of the lot and onto the highway.

"So give."

"Pie's meeting with an Office of Management and Budget delegation next week so Don and I were both in Pie's office pinch hitting for you. In the middle of the briefing, which we were getting pretty sick of anyway, Lenore rang in to say that Colonel Burnside was on the phone for Don."

"The staff's name for him is 'Call-me-Colonel. He's never going to make that grade."

"Well, whatever he is, he started to give Don an earful and Don put it on speaker phone. The bozo said you refused to show up at the normal 9:00 ack emma time and more than that, you refused to permit him to sit in on your interviews with staff and he wanted you disciplined for your insolence. What's ack emma?"

"It's a Britishism for A.M. Pip emma is P.M. I don't know why Burnside uses it. It isn't military-speak."

"How do you know these crazy things?"

"So what did Don say?"

"He said you were carrying out the assignment he gave you and he didn't see what there was to discipline you about. Then he asked him what his official rank was and Burnside admitted that he was a lieutenant colonel. So then Don said that translates to the civilian rank of GS13 or 14 and that you were a 15, so you outranked him. Then Burnside had a full-sized cow and demanded to talk to Don's superior, who was sitting there trying not to laugh so loud he might be heard on the speaker phone."

By this time *I* was laughing so hard I was afraid I could be heard in the next county. I held up my hand to stop Alex. When I got myself under control, I said, "You may proceed, sir."

"Then Don told Burnside that he would be happy to transfer the call and to hold the line. Then he took it off speaker and hit the mute button so we could laugh in peace.

"Once we subsided, Don pointed at Pie and said, 'You're on'.

"Pie picks up the phone and says, 'This is Dr. P.I. Lee, to whom am I speaking?' and the bozo says 'This is Colonel Burnside of USAO' and Pie says, '*Lieutenant* Colonel Burnside?' and Burnside admits it's him.

"What can I do for you, Lieutenant Colonel?" asks Pie. And Burnside goes into a tirade about both you and Don.

"So Pie says that since you outrank the bozo, it seemed to him that the insolence was all on the other side, and the bozo says that you were under his command at the USAO facility and that the military outranks the civilians in any case.

"Then Pie got mad and he tells him that, first of all, you were not under his command, you were a visitor to USAO and he had treated you with extreme discourtesy. Second of all, if he thinks the military outranks civilians, he should re-read the Constitution in case he missed the pertinent parts when he took Civics in high school. Then he asked for the name of Burnside's superior officer."

By this time, I was again laughing so hard that my eyes were tearing. "What then?" I gasped.

"Burnside started backing and filling. He said that maybe he had been a bit hasty and they came to an agreement and rang off."

"What agreement?"

"Pie agreed to trade you to USAO for Burnside and two players to be named later."

"You nut!" I reached over and started tickling him.

Prudently, Alex pulled onto the shoulder and grabbed me. He was about to make his intentions known when there was a knock on the window. A state trooper.

Alex lowered the window.

"Do you folks need help?"

"No," I said.

"Yes," said Alex, "this she-creature attacked me and..."

"Geez," said the trooper, "you're lucky I didn't have you fools towed."

He stomped back to his cruiser and Alex pulled decorously back onto the highway.

A middle-aged woman with a notebook and pen was waiting on our doorstep. "Ms. Goode, Ms. Goode. May I have a word with you?"

Since the woman was blocking the entrance to our house I had no choice. "Sure."

"I'm Penelope Benkard." She stopped.

I looked at Alex. He shrugged. Were we supposed to know the name?

"I'm with *The Examiner.*"

That sounded like a newspaper.

"I understand that you are working with the Army Observatory."

Oh dear. "I work for the Laboratory for Industrial Technology."

"Yes, but you are working with the Army Observatory."

I acknowledged the fact. "What is it you want?"

"How did you feel when you learned that one of the Observatory's staff had been murdered with a pumpkin?"

Alex turned his back. I deduced, from his shaking shoulders, that he was laughing.

"I was, of course, dismayed."

"Just dismayed? When your colleague was killed in that bizarre fashion?"

"Since this was my first day at the Observatory and I had never met the man, I think 'dismayed' was an appropriate reaction."

She snapped the notebook shut. "I must say that Ethel Goodfoot was entirely correct. You are one cold fish."

Alex unsuccessfully tried to stifle a snort.

"Ah," I said, "Ethel. I have no further comment."

"Is that all you have to say?"

"Yes."

Alex, my savior, butted in. "Excuse me, ma'am. But if I don't get to the bathroom immediately, something really nasty is going to happen."

Benkard jumped out of the way. Alex, key at the ready, opened the door and pulled me in. We made it to the living room, where we collapsed, laughing.

When sufficiently recovered I asked, "Have you ever heard of *The Examiner*?"

"Yeah. It's one of those throw-aways that clutter up the doorstep. I wouldn't worry about this. Their entire readership could meet in a phone booth."

So I didn't worry and nothing happened except that someone (now who could that be?) left a copy of *The Examiner's* story on my desk. It called me a cold fish. Not really headline material.

Chapter 3

October 9, 1991

The commute from our house in Alexandria, Virginia to LIT in the wilds of Maryland took about an hour. The Virginia Department of Transportation assured us that once the lawsuits were all settled and US 66 became a Virginia reality, commute times would be drastically reduced. Yeah, sure. Given the rate of population expansion into the boonies, that miracle road couldn't begin to catch up. So, we took the Interstate we had – US495 – hooked up with the country roads, and sat back and enjoyed it.

Alex and I parted in the parking lot. Since I only had one interview today, I decided to pop in and give Pie a quick update. Lenore announced me.

Pie was on his feet and shaking his head as I walked in. "Hello, *bubele*. No matter how many times I tell Lenore that she doesn't have to announce people, she does it anyway. What's with her?"

"Just tell her not to do it. If you tell her she doesn't have to, she thinks she has a choice."

"That simple, huh? What brings you here, the lieutenant colonel too much for you?"

"Not at all. I rapped his knuckles and he's pretty much stayed out of my way – except for complaining to you. Alex gave me a blow-by-blow. I'm sorry I missed it. The staff, by the way, has nicknamed him 'Call-me-Colonel.'"

"So aside from 'Call-me-Colonel', how's it going?"

"Going well. I've done all of the interviews except for Letitia Krackov and I'll get her today. It's a very small staff. I'm not going to have to spend all day every day there. Probably not all day any day.

"The astronomer is a transplanted Aussie. He appears to be a nice guy, but not much of an astronomer – anyone really good would be wasted there. The most they can do with that telescope is map nearby elliptical galaxies, and Doolittle is capable of that.

"The general factotum – secretary, dogsbody, human resources person if needed – is a young woman who intends to quit and have babies when the occasion arises.

"There's a marvelous post-doc, Bobby Figgle. He's extremely smart; the only reason he took this position is that Letitia Krackov is there and she agreed to mentor him. He declaims original limericks whenever appropriate and often when not."

"Why does he do that?"

"I suppose because he can. It's too bad he's not a computer guy. He'd fit right in here."

Pie looked around for something to throw at me. Not finding anything, he subsided. "Is that all?"

"Two more. Chuck Hadaman, the telescope engineer and king of the machine shop, is a gem, both professionally and personally. The guy who's supposed to be helping him, however, is another story.

At which point, Pie's phone rang. Lenore, announcing the arrival of Don. "Lenore," said Pie, "in the future please allow the LIT staff to come in unannounced, unless I tell you otherwise."

"Yes, sir," She hung up and Don walked in.

He gazed at me, crossed his arms over his chest, and said, "Didn't trust Alex and me to brief Pie, huh?"

"I trust you both implicitly. I've just been giving Pie a rundown of the USAO staff. I'm on the last guy, who is a doozy."

Pie said, "So finish up. Then you can admit that you don't trust them."

"His name is Tristram Gomping. He's a GS-7, supposed to be Hadaman's assistant, except he's never there. I suppose his job interferes with his extracurricular activities. For instance, he claims to be the musicologist for the local chapter of The Culture Club..." I noted the expression on Don's and Pie's respective face. "Not *that* Culture Club. This one apparently studies world cultures. I asked him what training he had as a musicologist and he said he was an autodidact. Then..."

"What's an autodidact?" asked Don.

Pie said, "Someone who's self-taught."

"A self-taught musicologist? Did he award himself a degree?"

"If he didn't, it's only because he hasn't thought of it. He also claims expertise in microbiology. I think he's hinting that he would like to be Pie's senior counselor, or something like that."

"*Oy*," said Pie, sitting down and crossing his elegantly clad legs.

"Which brings me to my first solid recommendation. The Secretary should insist that the Army abolish Gomping's job before the transfer is effected."

Pie who has been a Fed for only a year, asked, "Why can't it wait until the Department takes over?"

"Because he'll have bumping rights. He can take a job at the same or lower grade if his resume indicates he's qualified. Then the person whom he bumps can do the same thing until there is no one else to bump. The lowest person on that totem pole is out of a job. That wouldn't be a problem – except for the lowest person on the totem pole — if USAO were assigned to LIT. We don't have anyone he can bump. But Department-wide it could cause a problem."

"You just earned your pay," Don said.

"But won't the Army have the same problem" asked Pie.

"Well, I don't know if the Army has the same rules, but if they do, it'll be their problem, not ours."

"Spoken like a true bureaucrat." Ben had walked in unannounced and unnoticed. "Did Pie admit that he had Don and me in at the miserable hour of 8:00am this morning?"

"What on earth for?"

"He wanted me to give him some numbers for the OMB briefing, and Don because if Pie had to get up early then Don should get up early."

"He speaks true," Don agreed.

"So we three waltzed into the cafeteria and every eye in the place was on Pie."

I waited for it.

"It was rare for him to be Pie-eyed so early."

I stood up. "I'm going back to USAO."

I got as far as the door before I remembered that thing of no little importance.

"By the way, the exec officer was murdered the other day."

"*What?*"

I sat back down and explained the pumpkin murder.

"*Gevalt!* Do they know who did it?"

"Not a clue, so far as I know."

"Maybe we should abort your mission," Don said. "That sounds like a dangerous place."

"I'll let you know if the party gets rough, but I don't see that I'm in any danger. In the first place, there's no reason to believe that anyone at USAO had anything to do with it. And second, even if they did, there's no one there who knows me well enough to want to kill me."

My three colleagues laughed.

"Well, you know what I mean."

Don said, "So the guy got killed by a flying pumpkin, huh?"

"Yeah," said Ben. "He was squashed."

At that, I really did stand up and go back to USAO.

A police cruiser was parked next to the red pickup. An ambulance was close by. I pulled into a vacant slot, got out of the car, and ran smack into a cop getting out of the police car. He put out a hand to steady me. "Whoa," he said.

"What's happened here?"

"A nasty accident. Looks like some guy fell off the catwalk with an unpleasant result. I was just calling in for reinforcements. You work here?"

"Do you know who fell?"

"A visitor to the place. Do you work here?"

"Sort of. The Army is off-loading this facility to the Department of Trade and Industry and I'm here to help with the transition."

The cop held out his hand. "I'm Joe." We shook.

"I'm Bea. Are you sure it was an accident?"

"From the colonel's description, that seems likely. The visitor – name is Pottle – had made an appointment, which hadn't happened yet. This would be a screwy time to commit suicide. We'll have a better idea when we can get to the body. We'll bring the equipment to the bottom of the hill and approach the body from there. When you come right down to it, we don't even know for sure that he's dead, but I can't see how he could have survived a fall like that."

"What did Burnside say happened?"

Joe looked disgusted. "You mean the Army guy? Well, you have to understand that it was everybody's fault except his. Pottle seems to have entered the dome unaccompanied, climbed up to see what was there, opened the door at the top of the stairs, walked onto the catwalk, and tumbled off. Burnside blames the secretary. It was all her fault for leaving Pottle alone. I'm gonna have to talk to Burnside again and find out why there wasn't some kind of barrier, or at least a sign, to keep people off the catwalk. I can show you the set-up if you want. My reinforcements won't be here for a while."

I took him up on his offer.

As we entered the building, we heard Call-me-Colonel shouting "...and his blood will be on your hands. Remember that!" We saw his back as he marched toward the corridor. A distraught Lorrie was standing in the common room, tears streaming down her cheeks.

Joe paused to pat Lorrie on her back. "I'm sure it wasn't your fault, Miss. That Army colonel is in charge here and he failed to secure a dangerous place."

I put my arm around Lorrie. "I'm going to the dome with Joe. I'll be right back. Then if you want to talk or have a shoulder to cry on, I'm yours."

"Thanks, Bea. I'll wait."

Joe and I continued down the corridor and into the dome. "Look here," he said. "That door at the top of the stairs is open and it leads to the catwalk. The catwalk is real narrow and the protective rail has been removed while the repairs are being made. If you don't know the lay of the walkway, the easiest thing in the world to do is go up, open the door, take a step, and it's bye-bye."

I started up the stairs just as Call-me-Colonel burst into the dome.

"What do you think you're doing, Ms. Goode?"

Joe stepped out of the shadow. "She's inspecting the scene at my direction, Colonel."

"Oh. Well then, be careful," he called to me. He didn't sound as if he meant it and he went back out.

"See," Joe said. "No sign. No barrier. That accident was just waiting to happen."

I opened the door at the top of the stairs, stuck my head through the slit, and decided that my inspection would stop right there. I descended the stairs and we returned to the corridor. Joe peeled off at Call-me-Colonel's office door. "I'm gonna have another word with that pompous fool."

I found Lorrie in her office, crying.

"Lorrie, why is Call-me-Colonel blaming you?"

"Oh Bea, Dr. Pottle is dead and it's all my fault."

"Tell me what happened."

"I just did something awful."

"Start at the beginning, Lorrie."

Lorrie wiped her nose on the back of her hand and took a deep breath. "Dr. Pottle called about ten o'clock and said he could be here in about an hour and a half if Dr. Krackov could see him then. I checked with Dr. Krackov, who said that was fine, so I told Call-me-Colonel and he said to show Dr. Pottle into his office as soon as he arrived."

"I thought Pottle wanted to see Dr. Krackov."

"He did, but Call-me-Colonel wants every visitor to be brought to him first."

I was about to say that Krackov had no connection to USAO except for the office, but kept my mouth shut. No point in introducing a digression. "Go on."

"Well, Dr. Pottle arrived almost exactly at 11:30 and I took him to Call-me-Colonel's office, but he wasn't there and his door was locked."

"Does he usually lock his door?"

"Always, when he's not there. I think he's afraid one of us will leave a whoopee cushion on his seat or something."

The imagery was vivid. "Then what?"

"I really didn't know what to do. We waited in the corridor for, I don't know, five or ten minutes, maybe a little more and then..."

There was a knock on the door and Chuck stuck his head in. "Sorry, am I interrupting s-s-something? I just wanted to see if Lorrie is okay."

"I'm fine, Chuck, really." And she burst into tears again.

"One of these days I'm going to kill that son of a bitch. I s-s-swear it!" He left.

I found a box of Kleenex on the file cabinet and handed it to Lorrie. She mopped up tears.

When she finished mopping, I asked, "Do you know why there was no warning tape or a sign at the top of the dome stairs?"

"I do. My job description says I'm the safety officer, so I told Call-me-Colonel there should be a tape across the door but he said that might cause a delay if the workmen didn't have quick access to the catwalk and he didn't want any delays. He was sick of listening to trip-hammers. So instead of a barrier, he issued an order that none of the staff should go up there."

"And that was it?"

"Well, except that Chuck told him the same thing I did, and Call-me-Colonel told Chuck the same thing he told me. But he also told Chuck that he was sorry he ever authorized the repairs."

Oh great. That would have made things safer for everyone. "Issuing the order was the only thing Call-me Colonel did?"

"That's right."

"Go on with the narrative. You were waiting in the corridor with Dr. Pottle and then what?"

"We'd been waiting for such a long time that I asked Dr. Pottle if he minded waiting for a few more minutes while I tried to find Lieutenant Colonel Burnside and he said that was okay. So I started back into the main building and I heard Dr. Pottle go in the other direction. When I turned around he was opening the door to the dome."

Another knock on the door. This time it was Worley. "Are you okay, Lorrie?"

"Sure," Lorrie said. And burst into tears again.

"Come now," Worley said. "Nothing that jerk says is worth crying about. Or even listening to."

Lorrie said "I know. But it *was* my fault."

"Oh, crap! Accidents happen and that's all there is to it." Worley left.

46

Before she melted down completely, I needed to hear the rest of the story. Pie and Don were going to have a lot of questions.

"What happened after you saw him go into the dome?"

"I started back to make sure there was some light in there but I heard him say, 'I'll be stuffed...' and then the door closed. I think he was amused by our little telescope when he had such a big one. I figured that if he could see the telescope, he had enough light. So I dashed to the common room to look for Call-me-Colonel.

"But he was right behind me coming out of the corridor and blasted in that stupid parade ground voice of his, 'Loofus, where is my visitor and what are you doing out here?'"

The door opened. No knock. It was Bobby. "Oh, hello Bea. Hey, Lorrie – you okay?'

"Yeah," she sniffled. "Go write me a limerick or something."

"I don't have time. I'll be busy kicking that bastard's ass." Bobby swung around and beat it.

"So what did you tell Burnside?"

"I told him where Dr. Pottle was. Call-me-Colonel said he'd just been in the men's room and didn't I have enough sense not to let a visitor run around loose."

Locking his door to go to the men's room? When a visitor was expected? And staying in the men's room for over ten minutes? I stuffed my imagination back into the corner of my brain from whence it came.

"So Call-me-Colonel went to the dome and I went back to my

office."

"Then what?"

"He came running out of the corridor and by that time Worley was here. My door wasn't completely closed and I heard him tell Worley what happened. He said that when he went into the dome the slit was open, so he climbed up the stairs to the catwalk and looked around. That's when he saw Dr. Pottle part way down the cliff.

"Call-me-Colonel told Worley to call 911. By then, everyone had heard the commotion and were all in the common room, so I joined them. Worley told them as much as he knew. Then we waited for 911 to respond. When they did, Call-me-Colonel told everyone to go back to their stations except me, and he told me to wait right there in the common room. Then he took the ambulance guys and the police and went into the dome, I guess to show them where Dr. Pottle had fallen.

"After that, he came back out and called me a stupid broad for leaving a visitor alone and it was my fault that he had fallen, that my indefensible actions would be noted in my personnel folder, and Dr. Pottle's blood was on my hands."

Lorrie started to cry again.

"Lorrie, listen to me. You are not stupid and you can't be in two places at once. If that jackass had been in his office where he was supposed to be, this wouldn't have happened. He was probably hiding in the men's room just to make Pottle wait. He's exactly the type who would do that. And if he really had been in the main building and you hadn't come to find him, he'd have yelled at you for *that*. Don't worry, if he puts anything nasty in your personnel folder, we'll remove it before it gets to the Department."

Lorrie's sniffles gradually subsided.

"Besides," I said, "he ignored the warning of both his safety officer and his chief engineer and permitted unsafe premises. I bet the cops will nail him for that."

"Of course, you're right, Bea. It really was his fault. You know, I was just so upset that..."

Noise came from the common room. I peeked out the door. The entire staff was there, listening to a tall, skinny man. We joined the group.

The man was saying, "One of our men made it down the hill and confirmed that the guy is dead. He says that it will be easier if we take the vehicles down and approach from the bottom of the hill. The equipment we need is on the way now. Joe is talking to" he looked at a note on the back of his hand "Colonel Burnside now. Joe'll take the police car down as soon as he finishes."

The tall, skinny man left.

After a minute, Chuck exploded. "That fat-assed son of a bitch, Are you really okay Lorrie? You know this wasn't your fault."

Lorrie gave Chuck a teary smile. "I'll survive. Bea calmed me down."

Worley remarked, "I wonder what he wanted to talk to Krackov about."

"Dunno, She's my last interview. If she knows, I'll find out when we talk."

"I don't think she knows," Bobby said. "The last time I saw her she told me that he made an appointment but she didn't know why."

We milled around for a bit and finally dispersed.

I went to see if Krackov was in her den.

Krackov's office contrasted violently with both Lorrie's and Call-me-Colonel's. The Army had not only provided her the work space, but laid it on to a fare-thee-well. The wall between her office and the adjoining space had been knocked out, giving her a double office. There was a flag-rank desk and chair, a sofa, a coffee table, two upholstered visitor's chairs, and a mahogany table, just in case she didn't have enough room on her desk to spread out. As it was, she needed every inch of the flat surfaces.

Inside this amazing space stood a small, white-haired, erect woman. "Please sit down." She motioned to one of the chairs. I sat.

"I understand," she said, "that you work with P.I. Lee. Is that correct?"

I nodded, wondering where this was going.

"Do you think you might arrange a meeting? I've always wanted to meet that man."

"He would be delighted – he's a great fan of yours." That might even be true.

"Well," she clapped her hands together, "what can I do for you? And by the way, please call me 'Letitia.'"

I stifled a laugh and responded, "I'm Bea."

Letitia eyed me narrowly. "You're trying not to laugh. Bobby has a limerick about me, doesn't he?"

I hesitated. "Well, yes, but if you want to hear it you'll have to get it from him."

She burst out laughing. Not a refined titter, but a full-throated guffaw. "All right, what brings you to my door?"

"I would just like to know your impression of this place and its inhabitants."

"The Observatory itself is silly. It was asinine to build it and stupid to keep it as long as they did. It's only capable of low-level observation. At least the damn fools didn't put a serious telescope in it. You can't see anything exciting here because of the interference by city lights."

She went on to describe the staff. She had drawn the same conclusions I had, but more pungently. Tristram was a nitwit and a buffoon. Call-me-Colonel was a nitwit and a dangerous buffoon. And she didn't understand what had happened to the once-promising Worley Doolittle.

"He said that his brother died just before he came to the States and that he just couldn't get it together after that."

"Pah! He was using obsolete techniques the day he arrived in America. Judging from his early accolades, he wouldn't have used those techniques even in the early days of his career. He's just lazy. But he isn't doing any harm here."

"Is Bobby as good as I think he is?"

"Oh, yes. He'll be a great one."

"He can't believe his good fortune that you're mentoring him."

"Well, I was feeling noble about it until he arrived. Now I think I got the better of the deal. There isn't anyone in the damned building for me to talk to, and I was running out of gas with my memoir. Then Bobby arrived. He thinks I'm mentoring him, but he's really helping me with my book. Don't tell him; it'll dilute his gratitude."

I laughed. "Just don't let him talk you into including one of his raunchy limericks in the book."

Letitia looked pensive. "Maybe I'll use one in the acknowledgements. Can you write limericks?'

"I can give it a shot. If I think of one, I'll bring it in tomorrow."

I got up to leave.

As I reached the door, Letitia called after me.

"Make sure it scans!"

Chapter 4

October 10, 1991

Yet another gorgeous October day. Alex lowered the driver's side window and I did the same on my side.

Alex, in full throated, off-key tenor: "When a felon's not engaged in his employment,"

Me, in not-quite-soprano squeak: "His employment"

Alex: "Or hatching his felonious little plans,"

Me: "Little plans"

Stop for red light.

Alex: "His capacity for innocent enjoyment,"

Me: "'Cent enjoyment"

Guy in the car in the next lane: "Will you hold it down. I'm trying to listen to the news."

Woman on the motorcycle next to me: "You're exceeding the allowable noise level!"

Laughing, Alex and I raised our windows. The light turned green, and the cars behind us and behind that one, and so on, began to honk.

Alex said, "Do you know the definition of a nanosecond?"

"No, tell me what is the definition of a nanosecond, Dr. Carfil?"

"It's the time between when the light turns green and the dumbo behind you honks his horn, Dr. Goode."

We unloaded three boxes of cookies from the trunk just as Pie and Don strolled up.

"Hey, Bea," said Don, "did you bake cookies?"

"No."

"Then what's in the boxes?"

"Cookies."

Alex said. "I baked them."

"It's like Bobby Figgle and limericks," I said. "Only with Alex it's cookies."

Alex handed me two boxes and departed for his lab with the third. I handed a box to Don, walked to my government car and put the last box on the front seat.

"Is that one for USAO?" asked Pie.

I nodded.

"If you're coming to our office before you go to USAO, better lock the car. If it's something to eat, those *gonifs* in the computer labs will make off with it."

I locked the car and walked to the admin wing with my two superiors.

Arriving at Pie's office, we noted that Lenore was already at her desk. Don opened the box and held it out to her. "Have some cookies."

"No, thank you," Lenore said virtuously, "I'm on a diet."

Don had started to close the box when Lenore said, "Well, maybe one."

Don offered the box again. Lenore took two.

We entered Pie's office.

"Geez," Don said. "If we'd stood there much longer she'd have eaten the whole box."

"So how did yesterday go?' asked Pie.

"A visiting astronomer was killed."

"*What?*"

"It appears to have been an accident. The catwalk on the dome is being repaired. While he was waiting for Call-me-Colonel to get out of the john, he went into the dome to see what was there. He must have opened the slit to get some light, saw the stairs leading up to the catwalk, and climbed them. The railing on the catwalk had been removed by workmen, so when he moved out on the catwalk and took a step, he fell off. Unfortunately, at that location the catwalk faces the cliff and he didn't survive the fall."

"*Vey ist mir!*"

"Bummer!"

"Do you know who the visitor was?" asked Pie.

"His name is Larry Pottle. An Australian. He was in town for a meeting of pulsar astronomers and had made an appointment with Dr. Krackov.

"There's a rule there that all visitors have to be brought to Call-me-Colonel, so Loofus escorted Pottle to his office, but Call-me-Colonel wasn't there – despite the fact that Pottle had arrived almost exactly on time."

"What did he want to see Krackov about?" Pie asked.

"No one knows, including Krackov. He might just have wanted to pay his respects to her. She's an icon to the astronomical community."

"What makes her such a big deal?" Don asked. "Is she a Nobelist?"

"There isn't a Nobel prize in astronomy. Alfred Nobel specified five disciplines that would get awards and there are some weird omissions in the list. Astronomy and biology are left out, for instance. Astronomers and biologists have won Nobel prizes, but they've been shoe-horned into another category – astronomers usually get the award for physics, biologists for physiology or medicine.

"One of Krackov's students got a physics Nobel for work in cosmology. But Krackov herself hasn't received one. She does hold the NASA Distinguished Public Service Medal. That's the highest award NASA bestows on non-government personnel."

Pie took up the narrative. "She's had an enviable career. Early on, she wrote her Ph.D dissertation speculating on the structure of the universe. There were a lot of hoots and catcalls about that until observations proved she was right. She had literally established a new area of cosmology. She went on from there – made her mark in several other areas of astronomy. Remarkable woman." He grinned at me. "A little like your Aunt Bessie, huh?"

"Only in the professional sense. I can't imagine Letitia cooking a pot roast.

"I'm glad to discover that you're a fan of hers. I told her you were."

Pie cocked an elegant eyebrow. "And what were the circumstances in which that revelation was made?"

"*She's* a fan of *yours* and would like to meet you."

"Really! I'll call her. Do you have her phone number?"

I provided it.

Pie noted the time and said, "You'd better get your *tuches* over to USAO."

Therefore, I went out to my government car and drove the cookies and my *tuches* over to USAO.

I was driving past the scenic overlook, enjoying the scenery when a red pickup squeezed past and cut in front of me with nothing to spare. I slammed the brakes and went into a skid. The front passenger-side wheel came off, and the car came to a shuddering halt just shy of the yellow barrier tape and the vase of flowers. The wheel continued on down the road until it came to rest in a ditch.

I was sitting in the car trying to convince myself that I really wasn't terrified, when a sheriff's car pulled up behind me. Joe got out of the car and approached.

"Bea! Are you okay? What happened?"

"Someone in a red truck cut me off. I skidded and the wheel came off."

"Can you describe the truck?'

"Only that it was a red pickup."

"Holy cats," Joe said. "You're lucky the wheel came off. You might have gone over. That's what happened to some kid last week."

"Yes, I did notice the flowers."

Joe called for a tow-truck and retrieved the wheel. When the tow-truck came, he turned the detached wheel over to the driver, and ushered me into the cruiser. We followed the truck to the garage. Half an hour later I was back on the road and driving to USAO – grateful to the mechanics who hadn't secured the wheel on that government junker. Incompetence has its rewards.

I pulled into the space next to Chuck's red pickup.

Lorrie, accompanied by Worley, met me at the door. Worley was carrying a somewhat battered briefcase. He said, "I found this at the bottom of the stairs to the catwalk. We thought you and Dr. Krackov should have a look."

"Okay. Is she in?"

Lorrie nodded. "But wait a minute. What's in the box?"

"Cookies. Should I leave them on the table?"

"*No,*" they said in unison.

"If you leave them there and Call-me-Colonel sees them, he'll confiscate them, bring them back to his office, and gobble them all up.

"He's got an appointment later this afternoon – presumably at the Pentagon, but I think he's got a popsie in town," explained Worley.

Pause while Lorrie and I tried to imagine Call-me-Colonel consorting with a popsie. I, at least, couldn't.

"Can you put them in your office until Call-me-Colonel departs?" I asked.

Lorrie did so.

We knocked on Letitia's door. "C'mon in."

We trooped in and Worley explained. "This is Dr. Pottle's briefcase. He left it at the bottom of the stairs. Since he was coming to visit you, I thought you should take a look inside before I turn it over to Call-me-Colonel."

Letitia opened the briefcase and extracted the contents. It contained a thick sheaf of papers and an edition of the *Astronomical Journal*.

"Why that old bastard! These notes may be the life's work of Morgan Lazuli. How on earth did Pottle get his hands on them? Well, obviously that's what he wanted to talk to me about. Don't say anything to Call-me-Colonel yet. Leave them with me and I'll try to figure out what's what."

We got up to leave. Letitia said, "Don't go yet, Bea. There's something I'd like to discuss."

The others left. I stayed.

Letitia grinned a conspiratorial grin.

"Did you do me a limerick?"

"Well, yes. But I don't know if it's up to Bobby's standards."

"Bobby has no standards. Read it."

B. Figgle, there's something about you,

That caused me never to doubt you,

I taught *you* enough

And *you* taught *me* stuff,

This book would be far worse without you.

Letitia stood up and applauded. "You nailed it, kid. What time is it?"

I looked at my watch. "Almost noon."

"Good. Let's go to lunch and have a celebratory couple of beers. My treat."

An offer I couldn't refuse.

We both ordered soft shell crab sandwiches and Smithwick's Irish ale. The ale came first and we took a refreshing sip, or more accurately, a gulp. Good ale.

"Dr. Lee called me. He'll drive up with you one day next week and he and I can meet. Thanks for setting it up. He sounded like a *maven* after my own heart."

My mouth dropped.

She laughed. "A *maven* is an expert, a guru. It's Yiddish."

"I know. You and Pie will get along great. But no one else will be able to understand you."

"Pie?"

"For his initials P.I. But since he's not a mathematician, he spurned the Greek letter and adopted the dessert. It's organic and he's a biologist. Everyone calls him Pie. Even the junior staff calls him Dr.

Pie."

"And why the Yiddish?"

"His mother was Jewish. Where do you come by the Yiddish?"

"My family was Jewish. They came from Poland. Like a lot of families that came from Eastern Europe, they were processed at Ellis Island and the officials there couldn't understand their last names. No wonder since the names were mostly unpronounceable. So they were given the name of the town they came from – saved a lot of trouble. My family came from Krackov, so that's what I am."

"How did you wind up at USAO?"

Letitia smiled. "I'm an old woman, Bea. I'd been looking at the stars for lo these many decades and it was unlikely that I was going to make another heaven-shattering discovery. The one thing that I could do was to document my life and my work. Among other things, I could tell people what it took for a woman to survive and thrive in a male-dominated universe.

"I'd spent my entire working life on the west coast and I thought I'd like to see what the east coast was like. I didn't want to go to a place where eminent astronomers were likely to congregate because I just didn't want to be bothered. So, looking around, I stumbled on USAO. I hadn't realized what a backwater the joint is. I went from too many astronomers to no astronomers – poor Worley doesn't count.

"I was about to throw in the towel when Bobby arrived. And I'm happy as a pig in...well, a pig in mud."

I laughed. "How did you manage to get that great office at USAO?"

Letitia snickered. "Well, during my early flapper period..."

"Your what?"

"My flapper period. It was toward the end of that era. I met a handsome young lieutenant and we, uh, did the Charleston together. Quite a lot of Charlestons. And we've kept in touch all these years. He's a retired general now. Stuffy, you know. But I called him and he called someone. And my office at USAO appeared.

"Now, let me exercise the prerogative of old age and ask you a personal question."

"Fire away."

"I understand that your first husband was killed in an auto accident."

I shouldn't have been so quick to grant the prerogative. "Yes."

"What was he like? Was he anything like Alex?"

That's not so bad. "Not physically. Harry was a bruiser and Alex is decidedly not. Other than that, they are very much alike – smart, funny, thoroughly decent, oh, and great, inventive lovers. Most people can't find one spouse with all of that. I've been amazingly lucky to have found two." I thought for a minute. "I'm pretty sure Pie and Bessie fit the mold."

"Are you and Alex planning to have kids?"

Uh oh. I don't want to go there. "I can't. When Harry was killed in the accident, I had a miscarriage and lost some ovaries in the process."

"I'm sorry. I shouldn't have asked."

The soft shell crabs arrived, and we turned our attention to them.

When we returned to USAO, I went off to find Worley to see if my plans for the morrow suited his plans. He came in the outside door of his dome office as I knocked on the front door. He motioned me in as he took off his coat and hung it on the coat tree.

"What brings you to my abode?"

"I'm about to start the modified participant-observer phase of my investigation and would like to start with you, if that's okay."

"Course it's okay, but what is it?"

"It's when the investigator both participates in and observes the activities going on."

"Well, as long as you don't follow me into the men's room. How do we start?"

"First, tell me what you do and then we can decide how I might participate."

"First, I look at the sky at night. So on nights when I'm going to observe, the time I start depends on the time of year. Here in October, it gets dark around 6:00pm unless I'm Call-me-Colonel. Then it gets dark around 6:00 pip emma. But for normal people, I might come in around 5:00pm, and start making a finding chart."

"How do you do that?"

"There are official lists of elliptical galaxies and each one has a number. I've been going systematically through one of the lists. I get the coordinates for the next galaxy and make a finding chart from that information. The finding chart is a rough map of a small region of the sky. It can be drawn by hand or created using computer software. I do them by hand.

"Then I open the slit, remove the protective cover from the top end of the telescope and, depending on the weather, I either get to work or I reverse the set-up process and go home. If it's a clear night, I dial the coordinates into the control box – the box I showed you the other day – and the controls move the dome and the telescope, so that it's pointing at the galaxy I want to observe. The telescope usually isn't dead-on, so then I have to use my finding chart to make an adjustment to get it lined up. While I'm observing, I'm also writing in the logbook everything that's going on. The camera attached to the telescope is also working hard taking pictures of the galaxy. This goes on all night, with me looking and the camera clicking, taking maybe five or six pictures. Those pictures are transmitted to a little portable tape unit. When I'm done for the night, I put the unit near the Sun workstation in my dome office, ready for me the next time I come in.

"In the morning I do the scut work. I get the logbook and transcribe the stuff that's in there, stuff like the time, the galaxy number, the seeing conditions, the time of each camera shot, stuff like that. I also reorder the data so when it's time to write a paper on my observations I've got all of these transcribed notes ordered in the same way and I can start writing without having to scrabble through a year's worth of data to make a sensible manuscript."

"Can anyone do that for you?"

Worley grinned. "If by 'anyone' you mean 'you,' yeh. It'd take a bit of training, but yeh. And my future biographers will be grateful for the change from my handwriting.

"Anyway, after that's done, I load the data onto my Sun workstation here and it reduces the data to light curves, which are used for the paper. That may take a couple of days. You got all that?"

I laughed. "Probably not, but if all I need to know is how to transcribe the logbook, I'll quit while I'm ahead. But that doesn't sound like it will take up much of my time. Is there any chance that I can observe with you?"

"If you don't mind staying up all night, I'd welcome it. It can get pretty boring all alone. What happens is that I set up the telescope and make the adjustments and then I take the picture, move the telescope, use the finding chart to adjust it again, take another picture, and so on through the night. Those pictures, by the way, aren't snapshots. They're more like very long time exposures.

"It would be a big help if you could keep the logbook. I'll dictate, you write. I won't really know if I'm going to observe on any given night until I look at the sky. You still want to do it?"

"Absolutely. If you can start my training tomorrow I'll get here in the morning. All of this is subject to my husband's acquiescence."

"Good. If he agrees, it's a date. And a cheap date, at that."

I drove back to LIT wondering how to explain to Alex that I wanted to pull a few all-nighters at USAO.

As it happened that was no problem. Alex had always wondered what astronomers did, and he agreed happily that it was okay with him if I worked nights if he could keep us company. I told him that I was pretty sure it would be all right but I'd check with Worley in the morning.

We then got down to a more serious discussion. "Did you notice," said my beloved, "that Hallowe'en is coming up shortly?"

"Well, darned if it isn't."

Alex drove to the Party Store and after numerous arguments – some of them quite heated – we settled on our costumes, paid for our purchases, and headed home.

Chapter 5

October 11, 1991

Alex spent the drive to LIT warbling "Fair Moon" – one of Gilbert and Sullivan's lesser songs – and nibbling on my right ear. He stepped out of the car in full voice to the boos and raspberries of those unfortunate enough to have arrived at the same time as he. Crestfallen, he muttered, "Some day they will appreciate my artistry" and shuffled off to his lab.

I walked down the corridor to my office and found two of the biology techies standing outside my door looking thunderous. "Something wrong?"

"Damn straight," Ronald the male techie said.

"Goddamn straight," Donna the female techie said.

"C'mon in and let me have it."

"You gotta do something about Ethel."

Uh oh. Ethel was a world class pain in the rump. She thought she should have been given my job. About six months ago, she filed a nepotism complaint with the Office of the Special Counsel, claiming that Pie had hired his old friend, Bea Goode. The complaint neglected to mention that his old friend had been working at LIT for three years and Pie had been hired about a year ago. The Office of the Special Counsel took one look at the facts and sent Ethel a preliminary predetermination letter saying that it would not handle her case. She had thirteen days to respond, but never did so.

The reason she was assigned to me was because no one else would have her. She regarded her function as looking after the well-being of the entire staff, and to that end she baked innumerable leaden cakes topped by sickeningly sweet icing. She organized, or tried to organize, an all-folks luncheon every time someone had a birthday. And if you know techies, you'll know that what they want most of all is to be left alone to do their work. Ethel, however, had the delusion that she was beloved. I think one of the typists liked her.

I really didn't know what to do with her. DoTI's human resources department was under the impression that she was a computer scientist because she had an undergraduate degree from an insignificant college. But in a place like LIT, top-heavy with Ph.D's, she was out of her league. So I found tasks for her that, with luck, would keep her out of trouble. My latest try was to have her help Marge with publications. But from the looks of the two techies, my luck just ran out.

"What did Ethel do?" I asked.

"It's what she didn't do," Donna said.

"Ok. What didn't she do?

"She didn't edit our paper, she butchered it," Ronald said.

As the story unfolded, Ethel totally rewrote the paper, changing meaning and syntax, and when Ronald and Donna objected, she informed them that she, Ethel, was the editor and that was how it was going to be submitted for publication. She told them not to bother going to Marge, her immediate superior. Marge would back her.

I struggled to find an appropriate response and finally came up with one. "Oh shit!"

I thought for a few minutes. "Give me the original paper and I'll take care of it. Nothing will be published without your approval."

The two of them boogied off to get the original manuscript. I called Marge and described my encounter with Ronald and Donna. "Did you tell Ethel that you'd back her?"

"Of course not. This is the first I've heard of it."

"Why am I not surprised? Do you have time to edit their paper?"

Unfortunately, she had a waiting list. "I can ask Don to tap the Department, if it's okay with you."

It was very okay with Marge and I went in search of Don. On hearing the story, he added his "Oh shit" to mine.

"Two problems, Don. First, we need an editor for the paper. It doesn't need a subject editor, it's been vetted by their department head and she's excited about it. It just needs someone who can clear up the misspellings and the prose. I'd do it myself but I'll be pretty much tied up at USAO for the indefinite future."

"Give me the original paper and I'll find someone."

One down.

"The second problem is what to do with Ethel. If I try to fire her, we'll be tied up in paperwork for months and we still might not be able to do it. Which is the *best* thing that might happen. The worst thing is that she might claim that we're retaliating because of that stupid nepotism claim she filed."

Don interjected another "Oh shit."

"I thought I'd make her head of the library."

"What library? We don't have a library."

"I know. That's why she can't screw it up. If I tell her we're going to establish a library and she's in charge of selecting the books and magazines, she'll be out of my hair until she's ready to retire. She doesn't have that much longer to go. I'll tell her to start with the Government Printing Office publications and when she finishes making her selections from there, with hope in a year or so, I'll start her on the various technical libraries in the area. There are lots of them."

"Geez," said Don, "did you get your PhD from the Machiavelli School of Public Administration?"

He thought about it, chuckled, and said, "Go for it."

Next stop was Pie's office. "Hey, *bubele*, I talked with Krackov. She sounds like a great lady."

"I had lunch with her yesterday. She said you were a *maven* after her own heart."

Pie laughed. "Called me a *maven*, did she? I think we'll be friends."

"I'm starting the participant-observer phase of my USAO investigation and I'll be working some irregular nights. Letitia said that you'd drive up with me some time next week. But if I'm working on that eve,

I won't be at LIT when you want to go. Do you think you and Aunt Bessie would like to drive up this weekend with Alex and me? The leaves aren't at peak glory quite yet but they ain't shabby. It's a nice drive and you can scope out the terrain."

"Whoa. There are a couple of problems with that plan. Am I right that if you're working nights you'll be with the astronomer?

"That is so."

"And do you remember that the exec officer got himself murdered not long ago? You may be spending the night alone with someone dangerous. I know, he seems like a real *mentsh*, but remember what happened last time.*

"And aside from that, how does Alex feel about being left alone?"

"I think I've got the bases covered, Pie. Alex wants to keep us company when we're observing. Safety in numbers."

"Okay then, but I'd be happier if Call-me-Colonel gave you a battalion. I don't think the guy will bump off the two of you at once."

I gave Pie a peck on the cheek and departed.

I stopped off to give Ethel her new assignment. She was delighted.

"What's my budget, Bea?"

"We don't have one yet. When you get all of the must-haves, cost them out as best you can and that's what we'll request."

As I was leaving her office, she was calling GPO to have a catalog sent over.

---

*See *Me Tarzan You Dead*

I felt like a crumb for deceiving the woman, but I couldn't think of anything else to do. If I gave her an assignment with the least bit of authority – or presumptive authority — she lorded it over people. If I didn't give her an assignment with any authority she whined to everyone who would listen and to many who tried not to listen. Well, she had three years to retirement and if she didn't take it, we could give her another sinecure. I'd like to move her office to Siberia, but she would file another complaint and she'd win that one.

Passing the alpaca farm, I noted that the herd was wandering around looking cute. It's hard for animals that large to look cute, but they managed it. A little bit behind them were a couple of mounds. Standing on each mound was a much larger animal. To my untutored eye they looked like llamas. What would llamas be doing in a herd of alpacas?

I arrived at USAO, parked, and walked in the door, closely followed by the mailman. Lorrie was there to greet us, as was Call-me-Colonel.

"Well," he said, beaming at me, "I hope you're getting everything you need. Is your office satisfactory? Do you have sufficient supplies?"

Pie must have scared the bejeezus out of the guy with his implied threat to call his superior.

"I've got just about everything I need, unless you can rummage up a coat tree or a hook over the door."

"Of course, of course." Turning to Lorrie, "Loofus, make it happen now."

Lorrie trotted off obediently.

The mailman held out a packet of letters. "Here's your mail."

Call-me-Colonel scowled at the man. "Here's your mail WHAT?"

The mailman said, "Huh?"

"The proper way to address me is 'Here is your mail, SIR.'"

"Hey look, you want the mail or don't you?"

"Don't be insolent!"

The mailman dropped the packet of letters on floor, said mildly, "Screw you," and left.

Call-me-Colonel, looking as if he were on the road to apoplexy, bellowed, "I'll report you to your superior, you, you, you..."

The appropriate sobriquet was not forthcoming.

I looked at him. "I wouldn't do that. You'll just tie his superior up in paperwork and it won't accomplish anything. The Postal Workers Union won't let anything bad happen to him."

Call-me-Colonel took a deep breath. "Well, of course, if you think forbearance is wise."

He turned on his heel and marched to the corridor.

Lorrie came out of the office of the late Finance Officer, bearing a coat tree. Bobby approached from the other direction, a far-away look in his eyes. He hopped onto the table and declaimed,

> Postmen have hard jobs to do,
>
> Tramping through mud and through dew,
>
> Our guy won't defer,
>
> He would not say 'sir',
>
> All that he would say is "Screw you."

Letitia, who had been standing outside of her office, turned to me. "You see, I told you he has no standards."

I got the coat tree settled in my office, shed my coat, and hung it up. It looked much better there than slung over the visitor's chair. I admired it for a bit and went off to find Worley, who was in his main-building office. I told him that Alex was fine with our arrangements but would like to join us for our night sky-watching. Was that all right with Worley?

Worley was quite pleased. Here was another body to keep him company during his lonely vigils.

We went into the dome to begin my training.

Worley showed me the logbook which was sitting on a little table next to the computer. He opened it to the last page, dated last week. "The first thing you do, is to put the date and time on the next clean page. Then every time I dictate something, you write it down on a blank line under the date. When we get done, you take the logbook into my dome office and transcribe the notes. When you finish, you leave the notes in my office and return the logbook to the table."

"What happens to the original housekeeping data, the data that shows what the dome has been up to?"

"The control box records every movement and sends the data to a magnetic tape in the shed.

"The transmission, which is virtually simultaneous, goes over our network to the shed where the magnetic tapes are stored. There's a magnetic tape reader over there. That's the only housekeeping record we keep."

"May I see what it looks like?

"I'll show you on Monday. We've got enough to do today."

"Who is allowed to read the tapes?"

"Anyone with the user name and password. Our staff is so small that we all have the same user name and password so that if one of us is out for any reason, someone else can do it if it becomes necessary. User name and password are the same – Admin

And we proceeded to do quite enough. I hadn't realized how finicky astronomers are.

Chapter 6

October 12, 1991

Pie and Bessie lived in a small old house in the country, not too far from LIT. They'd bought it when Pie came to LIT about a year ago and suffered through the remodeling that accompanies the purchase of old houses. Walls knocked out, bathrooms put in, kitchen totaled and rebuilt. It now had fewer rooms but they were large and comfortable. Bessie's kitchen was glorious – the only drawback being that they had to use propane since the gas lines eschew country living.

Bessie was an eminent archeologist, happily digging her way around the world. But when she wasn't being eminent she was cooking up a storm. And in her new kitchen she cooked in everything from vented grills to made-to-order Etruscan-type pots. Did you know that the buried city of Pompeii had fast-food restaurants that contained counters on which food was served hot off similar grills? These were apparently for the hoi polloi who grabbed a *nosh* from them on their way to and from work. The wealthier Pompeiians ate sumptuous meals at home, cooked by talented servants. Dinner at the Lees was not only a gastronomic delight, but an education.

Pie and Bessie were waiting for us when we picked them up about

10:00am. Pie had traded his impeccable workday clothes for equally impeccable weekend attire. Sharply creased chinos topped by a beautifully tailored camel's hair car coat. He also wore a cute little cap. Bessie, on the other hand, wore the first thing that came to hand when she opened her closet. Just like Alex and me.

Shortly, we were on the trail toward USAO. It had rained overnight and the air was crisp and clear. The windows were lowered and all was right with the world.

As we passed the alpaca farm, Bessie said, "Whoa, there." I stopped and pulled over. "Those are alpacas," she said and got out of the car. A couple of alpacas strolled over. Bessie cooed at them and they cooed back.

By this time, we were all out of the car and approaching the fence. "Approach slowly and make comforting sounds. If they think you're dangerous they might spit at you, although they don't usually spit at people. They'll spit at one another if they're provoked."

"They spit like camels?" Alex asked.

"They're related to camels," Bessie said. "Also to llamas and vicunas. They're smaller than their relatives. These guys probably came from Peru."

"I think there are a couple of llamas in back of the herd," I said.

Bessie peered into the pasture and laughed. "I didn't notice them. I was so busy with the alpacas I missed seeing two four-hundred-pound beasts. They're beautiful, aren't they?"

"Yeah. But why are they there?"

"They guard the alpacas. The little critters are pretty defenseless. They don't even have hooves, just two toes. So they're vulnerable to stray dogs and any other kind of predator. The llamas are very protective of what they consider *their* herd. And they're big enough to take down a small bear, if need be."

"Amazing," said Pie.

When we had our fill of alpacas and llamas, we trooped back to the car where Bessie continued her instructional talk. "Unlike llamas, the alpacas were never bred to be pack animals. Their coat produces great wool – they get sheared like sheep. Pie has an alpaca sweater on under his jacket. If it gets much warmer out, he'll swelter."

Pie laughed. "That's the nice thing about jackets, they have buttons. You can take them off."

Bessie gave him a hug. "Alpacas also are very neat. They don't defecate all over their pasture. They pick a few places away from their normal pasturage. It's easy to clean up after them.

"That's why they make great, affectionate pets. You can housebreak them."

"No kidding," I said. "Alex..."

"*No! No alpacas!*"

"I'm not talking about alpacas. I'm talking about one alpaca."

Alex looked panic-stricken. Pie and Bessie started laughing.

"Look, Bea, we live in a little town house in Alexandria. Where would we put the damn thing."

"They aren't much bigger than a St. Bernard."

"Where would we put a St. Bernard?"

Pie and Bessie were convulsed.

"Look, we can get a small dog. How about a small dog? Or a cat. Yeah. A cat would be good. Maybe we can get one of those lop-eared cats. Or a Manx cat – you know, the one without a tail. They're supposed to behave a lot like a dog. Or a Maine coon cat. They don't shed."

"But they're not alpacas."

Pie and Bessie were gasping.

"But Bessie said they're affectionate. What if the thing wants to get in bed with us? You want an alpaca in bed with us?"

I couldn't keep it up. I started laughing.

Alex looked at me suspiciously. "Are you pulling my chain?"

"Yes, Alex. I'm pulling your chain."

I made sure no one was coming and continued up the mountain.

Every once in a while Alex started laughing, which set us all off again.

I drove into the USAO parking lot so that my passengers could have a look around. I didn't have a key, so a tour of the grounds was the best I could do. But at least Pie and Alex now knew how to get there.

The road past USAO was virgin territory for all of us. The farms gave way to orchards and, unlike the road up, there didn't seem to be any small towns, just occasional roadside stands and small markets. One of the markets had a sign boasting double-yolk eggs. Both Alex and Bessie cried, "Hey! Stop!" Nothing for it but to enter and purchase.

The store also contained a circular counter of bagged apples, each bag labeled with the variety therein. An apple-cheeked (of course), roly poly woman stood within the circle. There were bags of Empire, Red and Golden Delicious, Jonagold and Johnathon, McIntosh, Crispin, and Rome.

Bessie was astounded. "Are all these varieties grown around here?"

The woman laughed. "Not only grown around here, but in our own orchards. And these are just the ones that are ripe now. It's a little late for the Galas and Ginger Golds and a little early for the Yorks."

We bought two dozen of the double-yolk eggs and a bag of Mc-Intosh. We returned to the car, very pleased with ourselves, and continued down Blessing Mountain. Now, in mid-October, the apple trees were covered with fruit.

The road itself was a sinuous trail making the most of the changing leaves.

After about half an hour we came upon a Pumpkin Shoot and Corn Maze. "Hey," said Pie, "is that where the exec officer got killed?"

"No, that one was west of USAO. There are several in the area. Do you want to try the pumpkin shoot?"

Alex and Pie were enthusiastic. I was okay with it. Bessie thought we were crazy.

I drove on until I could make a U-turn, did so, and pulled into the entrance of the farm. A big kid with thick glasses and wearing bib over-alls shambled toward us. We got out of the car and went to meet him.

"You want the punkin shoot or the maze?"

Pie expressed our preference.

"That's good," the kid said. "I don't know how much to charge for the maze. You get five punkin shots for six bucks."

"Well," Pie said, "three of us want to shoot, so we each need five shots."

The kid thought. "My dad's not here. He went down the mountain to get some lunch. He'll be back in about half an hour. Can you wait for him?"

"Can't you take our money?"

"Oh, sure. I'm in charge here. But I don't know how much three of you will cost. I'm not real good at arithmetic."

"I see," said Pie. He turned to us. "Can we each pony up a five and a one."

With a little shuffling of bills, we managed to come up with three fives and three ones.

Pie went back to the kid. "Suppose we pay you six bucks when we take our turn?"

The kid lit up. "That would be dandy. My name is Jackie."

Pie introduced each of us and the kid shook our hands.

"Now, the way this works is that those bulls-eye boards about thirty feet away," he pointed at some bulls-eye boards, "are some of the targets you can aim at. And those a little further on are more targets. And then those way down are other targets. You can aim at any of 'em."

Alex asked, "What happens if we hit one?"

"Nuthin,'" Jackie said.

He continued. "See that little platform with the long thing on it?"

We nodded.

"And you see that box with alla the punkins?"

We nodded.

"Well, the first thing is that I got to turn on that other thing – it's called a com-press-or — and that makes the air go into the long thing. That's called a cannon. Then when it's your turn you climb up the stairs to the little platform and I put a punkin in the cannon and then you point the cannon where you want it to go. Oh, and I forgot to tell you, when you want to shoot, you pull down on that thing that's sticking out."

Alex, the engineer, managed to follow the narrative. "Maybe you should go first," Pie said.

So Jackie turned on the compressor, Alex paid his six bucks and the shoot began.

After the first shot, Jackie turned to me and said, "Do you go to work or do you stay home like my mom?"

"I go to work, Jackie. At the Observatory down the road." No point complicating things.

"Wait'll I load another punkin, then I got sumpin to tell you."

He came back. "The thing I got to tell you is that a fella from that place you work comes here alla time. He's real good at hitting the targets." He went to load another pumpkin.

"Do you know his name? Maybe I know him."

"No. I don't know his name. He's not as nice as you. He's nice, but he didn't tell me his name like you did."

"What does he look like?"

"I don't know because when my dad's here, he's in charge and I'm at the com-press-or. And I don't see too good. My dad sees even worse. He's blind but he gets around the farm good. Sometimes people cheat him, like they give him two ones instead of a five and a one. But mostly they give him extra money so it comes out sorta even."

"How does he get down the mountain for lunch?'

"My mom drives him. He don't hear too good either. He's got a thing he puts in his ear but mostly he forgets to turn it on.

"But I hear okay."

"Could you hear how the guy from the Observatory talked?"

"Oh sure. He talked real funny"

Pause for another pumpkin.

"Funny how?

"Just funny. You know."

And that was all I could get out of him.

Alex managed to hit three targets. He claimed they were the ones he was aiming at. Pie also managed three. I was lucky to get one – one of the far-away targets. Bessie, by this time, had decided to try her hand at it. She hit four. Go figure.

We climbed back in the car and continued down the mountain.

"So what do you think?" Pie asked.

"I think someone at USAO is a dead-eye with the pumpkin shoot."

"Who talks funny at USAO?" Bessie asked.

"Just about everyone. Chuck stutters, Worley has an Aussie accent.

Tristram can't pronounce the 'sh' sound, which would be noticeable at a pumpkin 'thoot.' Call-me-Colonel with his parade ground bellow. The only people we can eliminate are Letitia, Lorrie, and Bobby. And not even Bobby since he might break into limerick every time he hits a target. Jackie could easily think that was 'talking funny'."

As we reached the bottom of the mountain, a town appeared. At the near edge of the town was a log structure bearing a neon sign: 'Hamburgers And.' I stopped. "Are we hungry?"

We were that, so I pulled into one of the few remaining parking spaces. As I did so, the restaurant door opened. A little man in a lumberman's jacket and holding a white cane emerged followed by a towering Valkyrie – undoubtedly the parents of Jackie. They walked over to a truck about the size of a locomotive. Brunhilde opened the passenger-side door, picked up the little man by the armpits and deposited him on the seat. She closed the door, went to the driver's side, got in, backed out, and roared off. We watched, fascinated.

The interior of Hamburgers And matched the exterior. Log walls, dim lighting, fireplace, rustic-looking bar, uncovered and much graffitied tables. We took off our coats and slung them over the backs of our chairs. Pie's alpaca sweater was indeed splendid.

A middle-aged waitress bearing order forms approached as we sat down. "Whaddya want on your burger?"

Apparently the 'And' in 'Hamburgers And' referred to the accessories. We could have onions, tomatoes, lettuce, ketchup, mustard, barbeque sauce, six varieties of cheese, pickles, chili peppers, mayo, slaw, bacon, avocado, fried egg, and mushrooms. All burgers were nine bucks no matter what was on them. We opted for safety and ordered some combination of onions, tomatoes, lettuce, and cheddar. The waitress took the order, but looked at us pityingly. She had a table of wusses on her hands.

Her next question, "What kinda beer?"

Obviously fearful of being here for days, listening to the roster of beer, Pie said, "Do you have Sam Adams on tap?"

"Of course."

Pie looked around the table. "Is that okay with everyone?"

It was.

The hamburgers that followed were models of their kind. No little flattened strips of pseudo-beef, they were rounded, grilled, and infused with something wonderful. We decided that it was best not to ask the composition of the infusion.

The waitress told us that if we wanted dessert, there was a pretty good bakery down the block.

There didn't seem to be any sign indicating the name of the town. But we decided to walk around No-Name anyway. It was a miserable excuse for a town. No-Name was tired. We walked to the "pretty good bakery down the block" and found a discouraged little store with dirty windows and a few bedraggled cookies on view. There were quite a few taverns, a dispirited grocery store, and an off-brand gas station. Aside from Hamburgers And, that was it. The rest of the United States might have been recovering from the recession, but this town had given up.

We had a bottle of water in the trunk, so we washed four apples to *nosh* in lieu of dessert.

Alex took over the driving duty on the way back. He didn't believe I was competent to drive after a glass of beer. He was probably right.

We noticed Worley's car in the USAO parking strip and debated briefly about stopping and introducing Alex and the Lees, but decided against it. We were sated, tired, and wanted to get home.

We dropped Pie and Bessie off at their place. Bessie politely offered us coffee. We politely declined and headed back to Alexandria.

Alex said, "I think we ought to tell the police that someone from USAO is expert with the pumpkin cannon."

"Yeah. Maybe they can get more information from Jackie and his parents than I did. Will someone be at the station on Saturday?"

"Dunno. Let's stop and see on the way home?"

So we detoured to Bella Villa.

As it happened, the sheriff was in. He was a pleasant, middle-sized man in his late forties or early fifties. He seemed to be the only person in the building. His name was Sheriff Heflin, 'Sam to most everybody.' We described our mission and he ushered us into a little conference room, explaining that his office was too small to accommodate three people. He took notes while I recounted my conversation with Jackie.

"Oh, Lord," he said, "you got more out of Jackie than I ever could. And his old man is even more hopeless. But at least the USAO women are out of the picture. This is a bitch, pardon me ma'am, of a situation. That Army guy doesn't make things easy."

We commiserated with him for a few minutes. Then Alex and I made our way back to Alexandria.

We spent the rest of the weekend lazing around the house. Alex made cookies and I ate cookies — what else?

"You realize, of course," Alex said, "that if we don't get some exercise we're going to get very fat."

"What exercise did you have in mind?"

"Heh, heh, heh," said Alex. So we headed to the bedroom.

Eventually, our exercise complete, I wandered into the bathroom to take a shower. Looking in the full-length mirror, I decided that I had best establish a baseline before I outweighed my trim, fit husband. Here was a man who could eat a deep-fried hippopotamus and maybe put on a pound. If he had dessert.

I took a long look. Auburn hair cut short. Was there some gray in there? I looked closer. There was some gray. Should I get a dye job? Naw. What he sees is what he gets. Eyes, at least, were still green. Non-descript nose. Lines starting to form around the mouth. Not so terrible, if they're laugh lines. God help me if they're not.

I stepped back and looked at the rest of the package. Bust looked firm; waist narrow enough; knockout legs.

Alex stuck his head in the door. "Hey, you're one good looking babe."

But putting on a little weight. So we went back for more exercise.

Chapter 7

October 14, 1991

Monday opened to a downpour. Washington-area traffic slows to a crawl if someone so much as spits on the street, so we expected to inch our way to LIT. Our expectations were fully met. We had allowed an hour and a half to reach our destination and arrived weaving around many fender benders and one full-fledged accident. The hills were alive with the sound of sirens.

But we got there. We each grabbed a little umbrella and ran to our respective offices. Ben wandered in bearing a small bag.

"I snaffled a bag of bar nuts from the Fireside. I'll give them to you if you don't think it will be construed as a significant gift to my boss."

"Give. I'm only your pseudo-boss. You're supposed to report to Don."

"That is true. But you write my performance reviews. Will you give me a good review if I give you the nuts?"

"Only if I like the nuts."

Ben handed me the bag. Cashews coated with pulverized ginger. "They're good for an 'outstanding.' What's the Fireside?"

"It's a gay bar – been here since the '60s. I met one of your new colleagues there." He parked himself in the visitor's chair.

"Who?"

"Chuck Hadaman. He thinks you're a big improvement over the idiot colonel he has now."

I laughed. "That's damning with faint praise. And anyway, he's an idiot lieutenant colonel. I didn't know Chuck was gay."

"He has chosen to remain in the closet until he's out from under the idiot *lieutenant* colonel. He's afraid that military moron will make his life hell."

"He's probably right. I'd better save at least half of these nuts for Alex."

"He has a problem though. He made me promise not to tell you this."

"What, that he's gay? Why on earth would I care?"

"No, not that, *this*."

And Ben proceeded to tell me that the eminent recently-deceased-of-natural-causes Morgan Lazuli was also a closet gay. And Chuck was afraid that Lazuli's notes – the ones now residing with Dr. Krackov – might out him.

"The next time you see him tell him not to worry. Even if Lazuli's notes do contain that information – which is doubtful – Letitia is not a gossip monger. If she says something to me, I'll ask her to be discreet."

"Hokay." Ben, having subtly accomplished his mission, left.

He popped back in immediately. "Did you make any progress finding out about the pumpkin shooter?"

"Not so you'd notice. All we know is that the exec officer was killed by a flying pumpkin."

"You might say," said Ben, "that his life came to fruition."

And with that he left. Really.

I dealt with my mail, returned phone calls, and popped into Don's office. "Anything new?"

Don was standing in the middle of the room, dripping. He had just made it in. Unlike Alex and me, who park at the curb, Don has an attached garage. Which meant that he pulled out in dry comfort and thus forgot to bring an umbrella.

"Aside from almost drowning, the only news is that I got an editor for the biology paper. He'll call the techies with his comments.

"How does Ethel like her new assignment?"

"She's happy. Didn't even mention the biologists."

It being just a tad after noon, Don and I fetched Pie and went to the cafeteria for lunch.

Because of the lousy weather, there were more people in the cafeteria than usual. We looked around for a spot with three vacant chairs. We found one at a long table otherwise filled with assorted staff members. Don asked, "Are these chairs free?" and was assured that they were.

"We'll hold 'em for you," one of the techies said.

Pie surveyed the line of trays. "Is anything particularly good?"

"The meat loaf."

"The rhubarb crumble."

"Anything else?"

Silence.

We went off to find our meat loaf and rhubarb crumble.

Seated, I asked Pie if he was free the rest of the day.

"What's up?"

"This might be a good time to drive up to USAO and meet Letitia. This rain is supposed to last through the night, so Worley won't be observing."

Don asked, "Does the rain interfere with the ability to observe the galaxies?"

"It sure does," I answered. "If you open the dome your telescope will get drenched and you might drown – among other calamities."

Pie and the staffers sitting on either side of our triumvirate laughed. Don was unlikely to live that down for months.

By the time we finished lunch, Don was nearly dry.

Pie suggested I call Letitia to make sure she had braved the downpour and would be free to receive him. I made the call. She was there and looking forward to the visit.

Pie insisted on taking his car, rather than the government junker assigned to me. "How would it look if a *macher* like me showed up in that tin can?"

"But it's okay if *I* show up in it?"

"Of course. You're not a *macher*. You're just a lowly, just a lowly..." His Yiddish vocabulary failed him. "But you're a sweetheart," he finished. Then," Is *unmacher* a word?"

"*Nonmacher* is better. *Unmacher* implies that I was once a *macher* but for reasons unspecified had been *demachered.*"

Pie considered. "You're right."

Pie pulled his Taurus into the space between Chuck's red pickup and Burnside's BMW. We dashed through the rain for the door.

Lorrie greeted us, her normally friendly face hidden behind a noncommital mask. Puzzled, I introduced her to Pie and told her that I'd accompany him to Letitia's office.

"I'm supposed to usher all visitors to Colonel Burnside's office first."

"Is that right?" said Pie. "Just tell the lieutenant colonel that I declined the ushering. Where's Dr. Krackov's office, Bea?"

I smiled at Lorrie. "Do you want to do the ushering or shall I?"

"Let's give him a two-escort usher."

So we both accompanied Pie the full four feet to Letitia's office. By this time, she had opened her door and had heard most, if not all, of the exchange. I performed the introduction and Lorrie and I tactfully withdrew.

Call-me-Colonel appeared from the corridor looking like thunder. "Loofus, who was that? You know I'm supposed to see all visitors."

Not being sure that Lorrie's response would be fit for a family newspaper, I answered for her. "That was Dr. P.I. Lee. I'm afraid that he makes his own rules. If he has the time, he may see you before he leaves."

Call-me-Colonel glowered, turned on his heel, and re-entered his sanctuary.

I invited Lorrie into my office and asked her if anything was wrong.

"Wrong?" she growled. "*Wrong*? Do you know what that toad did? I'll tell you what he did. Do you want to know what he did?"

"Yes, please," I said.

Lorrie proceeded to tell me what the toad did. He called her into his office and told her he was concerned about her immortal soul. He went on to say that he was aware that she was not a Catholic and therefore she could not be absolved of the sin she had committed in causing the death of Dr. Pottle. He continued by advising her to take instruction in the Catholic faith, convert to Catholicism, and seek absolution. He then handed her a packet of literature.

I was dumbfounded. Among my extensive roster of Catholic acquaintances and friends, I could not think of one who would proffer anything that outrageous. And my friends included a couple of Roman Catholic priests.

"What did you say to him? What did you do?"

"If his freaking desk hadn't been between us, I'd have punched his toady face. Look, Bea, I'm a good Christian. We go to church most Sundays. We tithe. I don't need that worm giving me instruction."

"But what did you say to him?"

"I thanked him for his concern, and started to walk out. He called after me that he realized I was upset about Dr. Pottle and that he therefore gave me permission to leave.

"I went back to my office and threw his stuff in the waste basket. Absolution my Aunt Fanny! If I murder that miserable weasel I wouldn't expect absolution, I'd expect applause!"

She thought for a minute. "I won't really murder him. At least I don't think I will."

"So he really doesn't think he had anything to do with Pottle's death, huh?"

"I guess not," she said. "Geez, Pottle would never have fallen off the catwalk if Call-me-Colonel had ordered a tape put on the door or hadn't been playing big shot in the john."

I laughed. "You may want to rephrase that."

After thinking about it, Lorrie laughed too. But she declined to rephrase.

Then she said, "You know, it's kind of sad that Pottle's last words were probably 'I'll be stuffed'. You should say something heroic before you die."

"Are you sure he wasn't talking to someone?"

"Who could he have been talking to? No one was in the dome."

"Hmmmm."

We left my office and I went in search of Chuck.

It wasn't much of a search since he was sitting behind his desk scowling at a sheet of paper.

"Hey, Chuck. Am I interrupting?"

He looked up and grinned. "Yes, thank God. I'm filling out requisition forms. Why do they make it so complicated to order a simple screwdriver?"

"Because that's what they get paid to do."

I explained the participant-observer drill and asked if he was willing to put up with me for a couple of days. He was amenable, with one caveat. "Just be careful not to trip over G-G-Gomping. You wouldn't want to disturb his nap."

"I'll watch it. Do you think I can get a key to the front door and the out buildings? I wanted to show Pie around the place yesterday but we could only tour the perimeter. I doubt if I'll need a key again, but just in case someone from the Department wants a weekend visit, it would come in handy."

"No problem. I was about to go over to the machine shop. I'll make you one while I'm there. You can start your participant-observer stint by finishing this requisition form. I need a set of magnetic tip screwdrivers and a small electric drill. In the space where they want to know why I need them, don't smart-ass. Just tell them that ours are w-w-worn out."

"You're all heart, Hadaman. You make all the keys here?"

"Yup. One size fits all. The keys to all the doors are the same. Except, of course, for Call-me-Colonel's office. He had special locks put on his doors. Had them made by the Army so no one could sneak into his office and steal v-v-valuable secrets."

"With the same key working for all of the offices and the out buildings, aren't you afraid of someone stealing the computers or tools? I mean, anyone could get in."

"*Anyone* can't get in. Only the staff here and there aren't that many of us."

There was truth in that.

Chuck put on his slicker and left for the machine shop while I finished his paperwork and left it on his desk. I then called Worley and explained why I had come in so late. We postponed the magnetic tape reader session to another day.

I left Chuck's office and popped into the common room to see if anything was up.

Laughter emanated from Letitia's office. She and Pie must have been hitting it off.

Call-me-Colonel emerged from the corridor and accosted me. "Dr. Goode, please make sure that Dr. Lee visits me before he leaves."

"Dr. Lee outranks both of us, Lieutenant Colonel. Neither of us can tell him what to do. I'll suggest that he visit you, but no guarantees."

"Hmm. Well, perhaps I'll wait for him here and catch him before he leaves."

While we were waiting, Chuck came back. He took one look at Call-me-Colonel and asked me to come into his office while he checked my work. I docilely followed him.

He took off his slicker, hung it on his coat tree, and handed me my key. "I didn't want the horse's patoot to know I gave you a key."

"Good thinking. He's waiting for Pie to finish with Dr. Krackov so that he can waylay him. I'm going back to my office. I'll call Pie from there and ask him to call me when he's ready to leave. We can both sneakily depart through the outside doors."

And that is what we did. I don't know how long Call-me-Colonel waited for us.

Pie got the windshield wipers running, the car warmed up, and we made our escape.

"I take it that you and Letitia hit it off."

"Of course. We're both irresistible. I'd like to have her, Bobby, you, and Alex over for dinner. I'll have to check Bessie's schedule; she's due back in Peru sometime soon."

"You've met Bobby?"

"Not yet," Pie said. "But I got a full description from Letitia. When he finishes at USAO, I'll help him get a real job if he needs help. Unless he already has one waiting for him." He paused.

"Letitia did solve a weighty problem for me."

"Oh?"

"You may recall that we took my car because I declared you to be a *nonmacher*."

"I remember that well."

"Well, I didn't feel right about that, so I posed the problem to the eminent Dr. Krackov and she proved her worth."

"And her solution?"

"You are a *macher*. But Letitia and I are *gantseh machers*."

"I can't tell you how much better that makes me feel."

We drove on in silence while Pie negotiated a series of curves.

When we passed the trickiest of the series, I said, "Pie, Lorrie described what happened just before Pottle fell. She heard him say, 'I'll be stuffed.' She assumed that he was talking to himself about the telescope because it didn't seem that anyone else was in the dome. But I'm not so sure. Anyone could have gotten in there by just coming through Worley's outside door and then into the dome."

I explained about the one-size-fits-all keys.

Pie agreed. "Maybe we should look at the backup tape and see what the dome was doing. Do you think you and Alex can do that? He'll be able to figure out how to access the tapes."

"If Alex hasn't committed to something else, we can do it tonight."

Chapter 8

October 14 (cont.) and October 15, 1991

I parked the government junker and ran through the rain to our Mustang. Alex was inside the car, waiting for me. "Hah! You finally arrive. I have come for the rent."

"Have pity, sir. I don't have the rent."

"But you must have the rent."

"But I haven't the rent."

"Then I will have my way with you, wench." Pause for consideration. "But maybe we should have dinner first."

Another pause, this time for a snoggle.

Eventually, I came up for air. "Having your way with me sounds inviting, but it will have to be third on the list. We have to go to USAO unless you've made other plans.

"No other plans, but what's so important about going to USAO?"

"We need to lookay at the backup tapes to see what the dome was doing when Pottle had his accident." I explained about not being sure that he was alone in the dome.

"So you think it might have been an on-purpose instead of an accidental death?"

"Unlikely, but we should check it out."

"Have you floated this past Pie?" Alex asked.

"It was his idea."

"Then off we go. How're we going to get to the tapes?"

I held up my newly minted key. "This will get us everywhere in the facility except for Call-me-Colonel's office. We can stop at the Four Leaf Clover for dinner. That will give the Observatory staff a chance to clear out."

We had a leisurely dinner of Irish fish and chips, helped along by tankards of Smithwicks ale. Dessert was rhubarb pie. Qualitatively, the pie was a definite B+, a bit better than the LIT cafeteria's rhubarb crumble, which rated a B. Neither was in the class of the Sholl's Cafeteria offering, arguably the best rhubarb pie in the world. It added luster to the entire District of Columbia. By the time we had finished dessert, the rain had morphed into a fine drizzle and it was clear driving to USAO.

There were no cars in the parking strip, no staff in the buildings. We parked, sloshed our way to the tape shed, and entered.

"Wow," said Alex. He was looking at a rack holding six large magnetic tapes as well as a single tape mounted on a tape drive. There was also a minicomputer (a Vax) and what Alex told me was a degaussing machine. He explained that the degausser was for the purpose of wiping the tapes clean so that they could be re-used. The tape reader was almost certainly associated with the Vax.

"And the other out building holds a machine shop?" Alex asked.

"Yep."

"And all this to service a facility that holds about six people? Or does the engineer also take care of other sites?"

"Nope. Just little old us."

"That's incredible. Well, let me see what the Vax has to offer."

What the Vax offered was the likelihood that it would read the tapes.

"The way they probably work it," Alex said, "is that they're on a seven-day schedule – one tape for each day, starting with Sunday. So each tape is visibly numbered. If you look at the tape on the drive, you can see the number '2,' for today, Monday. So assuming that they do the setup at 8:00am, the astronomer or the engineer will remove the previous day's tape from the drive, put it on the rack, take the current day's tape, degauss it, and put it on the drive. That's Tape 2, which has today's data. Tomorrow morning, Tape 2 will be put on the rack, 3 will be degaussed and put on the drive. So – the tape we want is number 4 which should have the data from last Wednesday, the day that Pottle fell. And we're in luck because its degaussing time hasn't yet arrived."

Alex removed Tape 2 from the drive, substituted Tape 4 and entered the shared name and password on the Vax. He examined the list of files to see if he could find the one that would start the program. It wasn't much of a mystery – 'readtape.exe' did it. The machine began reading the drive.

It was the correct tape, but unfortunately the data on it were seriously corrupted. The reading would go on a bit and then there would be a blank patch. Then okay again and then blank. Unfortunately, the data we were looking for had been in one of the blank patches.

"What could have caused that?" Alex mused.

"Possibly Tristram Gomping," I hazarded. "He has been known to enter the shed with a toolbox full of magnetic-tipped screwdrivers."

"Not likely unless he was waving the screwdrivers around close to the tape. But odd things do happen. Let's look at some of the other tapes to see if they're also affected."

We looked and they weren't.

"You know," Alex said, "we should make a copy of tape 4 just in case it's needed as evidence if someone gets nailed for murder. We can copy it at LIT quickly. Are you up to going back to my lab, copying the tape, and bringing it back here?"

"That's a no brainer. Let's go."

And that's what we did.

Once we returned to USAO, Alex put Tape 2 back on the drive and the original Tape 4 on the rack.

We left the shed as we had found it and headed home.

This was not good. The almost certain conclusion was that someone had deliberately corrupted the tape and had forgotten, or hadn't known, to doctor the ones on the rack.

Tuesday dawned dry and clear. A windows-down day. For a change, albeit a temporary one, Alex had abandoned his beloved Gilbert and Sullivan in favor of Lerner and Lowe. I pulled into a parking space with my husband warbling, 'The Rain in Spain.' A few of his rowdy techies heard him coming and greeted him with 'We'll quit, Professor Higgins'.

We got out of the car and Alex snarled at them, "Boy, I'll never bake you Philistines cookies again."

"Oh no!"

"A cookie drought!"

"We apologize."

"That's better," Alex said and ambled off with his forgiven minions.

For my part, I headed to Pie's office and gave him the result of our snooping.

"*Gevalt!* That sheriff you talked to in Bella Villa, what kind of guy is he?"

"Seemed like an intelligent, friendly sort. A bit at sea with the pumpkin murder. Not surprising since his witnesses are either blind, deaf, or both."

"Let's call him and really ruin his day."

Pie asked Lenore to get the number of the Bella Villa sheriff's office.

"Shall I call them for you?"

"No, thanks. Just get me the number."

When the number was forthcoming, Pie dialed. Sheriff Sam answered. He listened carefully as Pie explained the situation. "Dad burn it!" Sam said.

Then, "I'm in over my head, sir. Is there any way you people can help me out? I mean, don't go looking for trouble or anything but if you happen across something that looks like it might be helpful, I'd appreciate it if you'd let me know."

"That goes without saying" Pie said then hung up. "It's a wise man who admits his limitations.

"Well, aside from that, Mrs. Lincoln....What else is going on?"

I told him about Call-me-Colonel's attempt to convert Lorrie to Catholicism.

Pie erupted. "That *shtunk*."

"Yeah," I said. "He's top of my list to be First Murderer."

"It would be nice," Pie said, "if the killer is caught soon, so we can get the Observatory moved and the staff out from under that excuse for a person."

"Does getting USAO moved depend on finding the killer?'

"Well, I'd hate to move it killer and all. But don't take it on yourself to go sleuthing. Maybe we should ask the Army for help. I'd better talk to the Secretary about that. I don't want to upset the negotiations for the transfer."

And on that note I took myself off to USAO.

Burnside was standing next to his BMW, some kind of wrench in his hand. His trouser knees were dirty. I got out of the car and asked, "Are you having trouble, Lieutenant Colonel?"

He smiled his tight-lipped smile. "BMWs do not have trouble if you maintain them on schedule. I am just doing a bit of maintenance. If you civilians were more respectful of your automobiles, even cars such as the one you drive, you wouldn't have the trouble you do."

What trouble? We drive a four-year-old Mustang and it's never given us any trouble. Don't start an argument, Bea.

"Do you do all your own maintenance?" I asked.

"Of course. It's the military way."

I left him to his military maintenance and approached the building.

Trip-hammers sang in the air. They sounded a tad fainter than they did yesterday. The crew must have been moving toward the back of the building.

Lorrie looked happier than she did yesterday morning. "I talked to my pastor," she told me. "He's really angry at Call-me-Colonel. He said the same thing you did about whose fault it was."

"What did I say?"

"That if anyone's at fault it's Call-me-Colonel's. My pastor is thinking about calling his bishop. But I don't think he'll do it. We're all being cuddly and ecumenical, so I don't think he wants to cause a rumpus right now."

"You're probably right. But it would be satisfying if his bishop would hit him upside the head."

Lorrie giggled. "Oh, and everyone wants to invite you and your husband to Bad Movie Night. It's next Wednesday. Not tomorrow but next week on the 23rd."

At last! Bad Movie Night to be revealed. "What," I asked, "*is* Bad Movie Night?"

"Oh, once a year NASA sponsors a meeting about Elliptical Galaxy Mapping. Astronomers come from all over the world to go to the meeting and this time it's our turn to host Bad Movie Night."

"Yes, of course. But what is Bad Movie Night?"

"Well, there's a committee that makes up a list of really awful science fiction movies. Everyone votes on which one is the worst and then they get a copy of the movie and they all get together and watch it on Bad Movie Night. The host – this year it's us – provides the beer and soft drinks in case some people don't drink alcohol, and everyone else has to bring popcorn."

"We can manage that. Do you know what movie we're watching?"

"I sure do. It's 'The Man Who Saved the World'. Sometimes it's called 'The Turkish Star Wars'. Some people think it's the worst scifi movie that's ever been made. I don't know why they've never seen it before."

"Well, I'm glad it waited for Alex and me. We'd be delighted to attend. Unless Alex made some plans that I don't know about. Unlikely since we always check with one another. When is it?"

"Wednesday the 23rd. At 7 pm. Better eat something first because all you'll get here is popcorn."

We parted and I went to find Worley for the promised session on reading the magnetic tape. I had no intention of telling him that I had already read it.

While Worley and I walked to the shed, he basically repeated what Alex had already explained.

As we entered the shed, Worley remarked that he had already degaussed the tape on the drive so there would be nothing for the reader to read.

"Let's get another tape." I plucked a seemingly random tape off the rack.

"That's number 4." He replaced the degaussed tape with tape 4 and fired up the Vax. He got the same result as Alex had. "What the hell!

"That idiot Gomping! Lorrie saw him going into the shed with a load of magnetic-tipped screwdrivers. He screwed up the whole tape. Well, at least you saw how it works. I'm going to show that tape to Chuck. Maybe now he'll get rid of that moron."

He put the tapes back in their right order.

We parted at the main building. Lorrie met me as I entered. "Dr. Lee asked me to tell you to call him."

I made the call from my office. "What's up?"

"Letitia and Bobby are coming for dinner this Saturday. Alex said he was pretty sure that you two could join us, but to check with you."

"We'd love to come." So Bobby would be there too. I guess Pie and Letitia decided that spouting limericks did not constitute "talking funny."

I drove back to LIT, scooped up Alex, and headed for home.

The next morning, we figured that the time was ripe. We left a bit early, having put our Hallowe'en costumes in the back. At the edge of the LIT parking lot, we suited up and pulled into a parking place. The trap was now baited and we waited and watched for Don. "Here he comes," warned Alex.

I leaned back against the door. My head, with its wig of golden locks, was hidden from view. Alex was bent over me. Right on cue, Don tapped on the window. Alex rose up and turned, his hands held at shoulder level and gave Don a full-face view of The Vampire, blood dripping from his fangs. I sat up, my yellow curls bobbing, my hand to my throat. Don gave a strangled cry and jumped back. Then, realizing that he'd been had, started laughing. Techies from both divisions came over to see what they could see. They all started laughing. At which point, Ethel the Useless walked by. She snorted, "Other people don't have lunatic senior management."

After Ethel came Lenore. "Honestly!" she said.

Pie arrived shortly after Lenore. He took one look at us and broke up.

Alex and I shed our costumes and got out of the car. Alex addressed the multitude, as follows:

> It was a dark and stormy night. A luscious young woman
> was driving through the Transylvanian mountains when
> her car stopped. Looking at the gauge, she realized that
> she was out of gas. She waited in the car for a bit and
> finally admitted that it was unlikely that anyone would
> be driving that way. But up ahead she saw a castle with
> lights in the windows. There was nothing she could do,
> but hoof it. After nearly half an hour, she arrived at the
> castle, cold and wet. She knocked on the door, which
> swung silently open. She entered. Looking first left and

then right, she saw a large room with a roaring fire in the fireplace. She sank onto a sofa and soon fell asleep. She awoke with a start to find a vampire standing over her. She leapt from the sofa and ran to an interior door. She opened the door; she closed the door. He opened the door; he closed the door. She ran through the room to another door. She opened the door; she closed the door. He opened the door; he closed the door. Yet another room. She opened the door; she closed the door. He opened the door; he closed the door. Finally, she came to a staircase and ran up, only to find that the door at the top of the stairs was locked. She looked back to see the vampire slowly approaching. Then she remembered that she was wearing a cross. She pulled the cross from her bodice and confronted the vampire with it. And the vampire chuckled and said, "It vouldn't voik, goily."

General laughter except for one of the biology techies. "I don't get it," she said.

Pie said gently, "It was a Jewish vampire."

She digested this and started to laugh, together with a few other techies who hadn't gotten it either.

I arrived at my office to find a sugar coated cupcake sitting on my desk. I had no sooner sat down than Jim Daley walked in carrying another cupcake. He handed it to me.

"Don't eat the cupcake on your desk," he advised. "Ethel has loaded it with something nasty. Give it to me and I'll dispose of it appropriately."

"Thanks, Jim. But there was no chance that I would eat something Ethel baked. How do you know it's doctored?"

"Ethel told us. She thinks we share her dislike of you. The dumb-head couldn't be wronger." He left.

There was no question about it. I was a coward. I had to do something about Ethel. True, if I did the right thing and fired her instead of shifting her around and annoying the rest of the staff, I'd be tied up in paperwork for months. Well, let it slide for a while. Maybe it will sort itself out.

Meanwhile, I could hide at USAO.

I had packed a chicken, lettuce, and tomato sandwich for lunch. I found Chuck in his office, told him that I was going to eat in and asked when it was convenient to observe him.

"I've got a sandwich, too. If we eat together, you can observe me m-m-munching."

We moved to the refectory table with a short stop at the water cooler. Lorrie joined us at the table. She not only brought lunch but had a large thermos of coffee. She made the mistake of offering us some. We took her up on the offer. Coffee-less people at lunchtime have no shame.

When we'd finished lunch and cleared the table of debris, Chuck and I repaired to his office, where he gave me an introductory briefing.

"Participating and observing for a couple of d-d-days isn't going to give you the full flavor of what I do because we're on a maintenance schedule and you'll only see the slice where we are now. I'll describe the whole enchilada, and then you can see what you can see.

"We do our maintenance more frequently than normal b-b-because the Army was being penny-wise. They bought the telescope and the mount new, but they got the dome from a decommissioned DoD facility somewhere out west, although nobody will tell us what it did out there. Trouble is, it sat around unused for a long time without anybody taking care of it, with the same r-r-result that you'd get if you bought a used car that had been sitting around for years. It needs more tender, loving care than most.

"So here's what we do. Every day we check his logbook to see if Worley was observing the p-p-previous night. If he was, we check the magnetic tape to see if there were any problems. If there were, we fix them."

"Let me interrupt for just a minute," I said. I told him about the corrupted tape and Worley's conclusion that Gomping was the culprit. Chuck's conclusion was the same as Alex's. He didn't think that just bringing magnetic-tipped screwdrivers into the shed would corrupt the tapes.

I didn't mention that only one tape had been corrupted.

Chuck went on with the briefing.

"If there has been recent precipitation, like yesterday, I walk around the dome to check for leaks. If I can find Gomping, I have him do it. If there's frozen precipitation – we'll probably get some in the next few months — we'll wait until it has completely stopped and then make sure that all the moving parts are working smoothly."

I stifled a laugh.

"What?"

I told him Don's question about whether it was okay to observe in a downpour. Chuck also found it funny.

"To continue. Every week we look at the dome rollers, motors, and drivetrains for wear. At the first sign of wear, we requisition a replacement. We don't wait. It takes so long to get the replacement after the form is turned in, the whole dome could collapse while we wait. I used to have G-G-Gomping fill out the forms but he turned them in at his convenience. So now I do them. Which is exactly what he hoped would happen.

"Then once a year we lubricate all the gears and bearings. If any of them should fail — and they could-do b-b-because they'd been unattended during the cold Western winters — I'd replace any damaged parts that make themselves known."

"How can you tell?"

"Well, if we hear a banshee wail when the dome is turning, that would be a clue.

"Then, aside from tending to the telescope and dome, I'm responsible for taking care of the buildings and parking strip. There's a little more to do now because of the repairs to the c-c-catwalk, but usually it's just making sure that the temperature is right to keep the magnetic tapes happy, and fixing whatever is broken in the main buildings. Things like the water cooler, the building's heating and air conditioning, or even flooring get out of whack. I check it all out once a year and fix whatever is f-f-fixable. If anything goes wrong in between times I can tell right away."

"How?"

Chuck laughed at me. "I get too hot or too cold, get hot water out of the cooler, or break my ankle tripping on a loose floor tile."

"You're brilliant, Sherlock."

"So c'mon, let's look at the repair crew and then t-t-tomorrow we can take a full tour."

We got our coats and entered the dome. Chuck opened the slit (an activity that was duly recorded on the backup tape) and climbed the stairs to the catwalk.

"Be very careful, this isn't fully repaired. You're Call-me-Colonel's ticket out of here. We don't want anything to cause a delay."

"And here I thought you loved me for my big blue eyes alone."

"Are your eyes blue?"

"No, they're green. But "blue" sounds better in this context."

The dome had stopped turning and the slit had opened right where work was in progress. We stuck our heads through the slit. A substantial metal pole sat on the catwalk. It was attached to the building by a hook and chain. Attached to the chain was a harness like those that window washers use and attached to the harness was a guy who had been lowered to inspect the underside of the catwalk. He was waving vigorously, evidently a signal to haul him up because another guy started pulling on the chain.

Chuck beckoned to a third guy, this one apparently the foreman.

"Anything to report?"

"A minor crack in the cement a little ways back. Iggy took a Polaroid of it. Let me know if you want it repaired." The foreman reached in his satchel and brought out a picture. He handed it to Chuck. Chuck took it and we popped our heads back into the dome.

Chuck said, "When they get finished, or think they're finished, I'll inspect the whole thing. For a lot of the catwalk, I can do the inspection by walking around on the ground and looking up. But once we get to the part where the catwalk hangs over the precipice, I'll have to get in the harness."

"Whew. Better thee than me."

Chuck closed the slit and we parted.

Chapter 9

October 15 (cont.) and 16, 1991

I drove back to LIT, went to my office, and cleared up some of the detritus that had accumulated on my desk. The biologists stopped by, proclaimed satisfaction with the new editor, thanked me profusely, and asked when I'd be back full time.

"Just as soon as I finish making the world safe for democracy."

"That long, huh?" They left.

Jim Daley arrived and closed the door. "My appropriate cupcake disposal was a smashing success." A broad smile creased his face.

"How did you dispose of it?"

"Ethel always leaves one on her desk for eating later. I substituted the one intended for you."

"Do I want to know what happened?"

"Well, if it were me, I'd want to know. But you're a nicer person than I am so I'll tell you whether you want to know or not.

"Ethel must have eaten the cupcake about ten minutes after you left. About an hour after that she busted out of her office and ran to the john. We heard her emptying herself from both ends for maybe twenty minutes. Came out of the john looking even worse than she usually does. Which is saying something. She went home right away."

I tried, without success, to look solemn. "That really isn't funny, except that it is. Thanks for warning me."

"Why don't you fire her? She's not just useless, she's a menace."

"You want me to put you in charge of the resulting paperwork?"

"Oh. I see." Jim departed.

I had to wait a few minutes while Don wound up his phone call. He was remonstrating with a soccer mom who was insisting that her little darling had not deliberately kicked a teammate in his gonzos and should therefore be reinstated in the lineup.

When Don finished telling me the details of the errant (or not so errant) kick I told him about the tape. I forbore to mention the cupcake caper.

"Alex and I snuck the tape back to LIT, copied it, and snuck it back to its rack at USAO. We thought we should keep a copy before it gets degaussed. Just in case it becomes evidence."

Don looked at me speculatively. "The Secretary was probably right. This assignment will be good for your career. But I don't want to lose you."

"The feeling is mutual. I'll turn down any offer of a Senior Executive Service slot. I want to stay here."

Don thought for a bit. "You know we have a vacant SES slot here. Pie didn't want to fill it. Said we had too many chiefs now. Maybe we can slide you into the vacancy."

"On what pretext?"

"On the pretext that we're going to solve this damn thing and the Secretary will owe you. Pie can slide it through."

"But then I won't be reporting to you and we've got a good thing going."

"Do you think I'm under the delusion that you report to me now?"

We both laughed.

Don gave me a hug. "Well, let's solve it first and then we'll see."

I removed myself from Don's office and met Alex at the car.

We stopped at the public library on the way home and looked up 'alpaca' in the various encyclopedias. The purpose of this being to dazzle Bessie with our encyclopedic knowledge of the beasts. They really are interesting animals. For instance, they only have one set of teeth – the bottom layer – in the front of their mouths. They have the normal two sets in back. When they close their mouths, the bottom front teeth rest against a top pad. Most of them also love apples. We therefore made a quick stop at our local grocery store.

The store was a throwback to the days when a grocery store was a grocery store. There were three steps down to the interior. There was a counter with an up-to-date cash register. To the immediate right were bins containing a number of types of potatoes and onions. To the immediate left were displays of bread and rolls. Behind the cash register were floor-to-ceiling shelves containing canned goods, alphabetized in descending order. If you wanted canned applesauce or asparagus the clerk took a long pole with a grabber on top and fetched it down for you. If you wanted canned zucchini, he got down on his knees and fetched it up for you.

To the left, past the bread and rolls was a refrigerator with dairy products. Beyond that were shelves containing everything edible in the civilized world.

The fresh fruit and vegetables were to the right of the potatoes and onions. This was where the bags of apples could be found. The variety of apples changed from week to week and you took what they had. One week they might have Cortlands, another week Crispins. But in any given week, there would be only one variety. Since it was unlikely that the alpacas could tell one variety from another, we bought four bags of whatever.

The grocery store is just a couple of blocks from our little row house in Old Town Alexandria. The house had been Alex's when we were married not quite a year ago. Since his house was much more comfortable than mine, that's the one we kept. We turned one of the two upstairs bedrooms into a shared study. A kitchen/dining room is downstairs, along with a living room and a small foyer. A great little house for living and cooking and so on. But not so hot for entertaining. Well, that's what restaurants are for. And Alexandria has plenty of those. Some of them are even good.

The neighborhood itself is wonderful. We're far enough away from the King Street nuttiness so that the noise of traffic doesn't intrude, and we can walk to essential destinations such as the grocery store without fear of being run over by gawking tourists.

Alexandria is a particularly dog-friendly town. There are many well-tended, fenced, pocket-sized dog parks where dogs can run around doing what dogs do. One of the hotels even has a weekly happy-hour for dogs. Alexandrians can be a little screwy. In other words, the place suits us.

The next morning we stopped at the alpaca farm, debarked, and got the apples from the back seat. We arrived at the fence and whistled for the animals. I don't know if it was the whistle or the smell of apples, but something caused the herd to come. It also summoned the llamas and a farmer.

"I noticed that you folk have stopped here a few times now. Thinkin' of starting an alpaca farm?"

"No," said Alex, "we live in a townhouse in the city. My wife wants one as a housepet."

"Oh," said the farmer, "that's not a real good idea. First of all, they're herd animals. Now you wouldn't need a whole herd, but you would need more than one or two or you'd have a sorrowful pet. Now second, they need someplace to graze. I don't imagine you run to pasturage in a townhouse. And third, they're real affectionate. You might find them in bed with you."

I asked, "Have any of your alpacas ever crawled into your bed?"

"Oh, no," the farmer answered. "I got better things to do in bed than pet an alpaca."

Meanwhile, the alpacas were looking at the bags of apples and making sounds somewhere between a coo and a hum.

"Better dump those apples over the fence," the farmer advised. "I think those fellas might be getting antsy."

We performed the dump and prepared to re-enter the car.

"You come back any time you want. If you bring apples, the herd will greet you before you ever get to the fence."

We waved good bye and continued up the road.

I stopped in my office, answered the phone calls that had appeared overnight, asked Don if he needed me for anything (he didn't), and walked to Pie's office. He reminded me that he would be locked up all afternoon with the OMB grill team.

"Will Freddie be there?"

"I don't know," Pie said. "I hope so. Have you got any advice?"

"I think Don and Alex have everything covered. Are you going to do this alone or will you bring in some of the staff?"

"I'll go it alone. If they've got questions I can't answer, I'll send for someone. No point in providing more targets for them to aim at if I don't have to."

I nodded. "Good move. Should I stick around?"

"I don't think that's necessary. If something comes up that requires your *seykhel*, we'll call you at USAO and put you on the speaker phone."

"Okay. Did Don tell you about the corrupted tape?"

"He did. This is *tsuris* up the *tuches*."

"It is that. I still can't believe that I'm in any danger, but..."

"Do you want me to yank you?"

"No. At least not yet. I don't think anyone there would regard me as a threat."

"Okay. But if this goes on much longer, you're outta there."

I nodded. "I'll drive up the hill now. Unless you have something you want me to do."

"No, if I need anything I'll call you."

From Pie's office I went to see if Ethel had managed to get into trouble with her library assignment. She was looking a bit peaked.

"Did you get the GPO catalog?'

"Yes. There's an awful lot of publications in it."

I concurred. "It's hard to have a library without a lot of publications."

"Do you think we need all the garbage that Kay and Kramer did for the Office of Telecommunications Policy?"

"It's your call, Ethel. If you want my advice, I'd leave it in and if it turns out that the budget calls for some pruning, you can cut stuff then."

Ethel nodded sagely. "That's just what I was thinking.

"By the way, I think we should organize a softball team. LIT should have a softball team. It would really lift morale. The staff at GSA really love playing softball."

Oh, dear. Doesn't this woman ever stop?

"I don't think we should do anything that important without Pie's okay. I'll ask him the next time he's free."

Except for the noise of the trip-hammer, everything was quiet at USAO.

Chuck was in his office, waiting for me. "This is the day we're scheduled to check the rollers, motors, and d-d-drivetrains. Gomping is supposed to help with that, so we probably won't see him until it's all done. Let's go get the ladders."

We walked out to the machine shop, selected two tall ladders, and loaded them onto a hand truck made for the purpose. Chuck told me that he had fabricated the truck right there in the shop.

"Do you have time to do that kind of thing?"

"I don't have all that much to keep me busy. I'd go n-n-nuts if I just sat around all day doing nothing. I don't know how Gomping does it."

"I believe most of his time is spent thinking deep thoughts."

Chuck handed me a tool box and a logbook. "Is that too heavy for you to carry?"

"I can manage."

We rolled the ladders through the corridor and into the dome. Then we set them up side by side at the dome wall.

"Now," said Chuck, "we climb up the ladders. Those things that look like huge roller skate wheels are the rollers. You have two tasks. One is to watch what I'm doing so if you're ever t-t-trapped in a dome with a ladder and rollers you will have something to do with your time."

"You ain't funny, Hadaman."

"Sure I am." Chuck laughed. "By the way, you aren't afraid of h-h-heights, are you?"

"I thought you'd never ask. No, I'm not afraid of heights."

"In that case we're good to go. Your other task is to take notes in my log from my d-d-dictation and to hand me tools when I ask for them."

We climbed up the ladders and began the inspection.

We went roller by roller. Chuck inspected each one and pronounced it good. We then went on to the motors where, with Chuck's guidance, I removed the covers and safety screens. He inspected the drive belts, asked for the oil can to lubricate what he told me were called 'bushings,.' inspected the gear teeth for wear, checked the brushes on the motors, and had me replace the covers.

As we went along, Chuck commented on what might go wrong. For instance, the mechanism might have rust caused by a leak, or there might be metal filings from metal-on-metal contact, or uneven wear patterns. I recorded the results of each inspection in the logbook.

When we had finished the inspection of the dome mechanisms, we went on to look at the mechanisms associated with the telescope itself.

"I'm a nitpicker," Chuck explained, "by nature and by profession. I treat every one of these inspections as crucial. When you slack off on them, truly bad things can happen."

The last thing we did was to go over the logbook and make note of what things had to be ordered. My final task was to fill out the requisition forms.

By now, it was time for lunch. Neither Chuck nor I had brought any sustenance, so we discussed the available food venues. The Four Leaf Clover was too expensive. Hamburgers And was too far. That pretty much ran me out of suggestions. Chuck said that there was a funky kind of pub in Bella Villa. It was a good place to eat only if you liked Welsh rabbit. The rest of the food was marginally edible. We had just decided on the Welsh rabbit when Gomping appeared.

"I am simply famithed," he announced.

"Bea and I were just g-g-going to lunch. You can go as soon as we get back. While you're waiting, get the ladders on the truck and wheel them back to the machine shop. Put them where they belong next to the other ladders."

Gomping was open-mouthed. "You want *me* to do that?"

"No," Chuck said. "I don't *want* you to do it. I'm telling you to do it. Bea and I will be discussing the transition to DoTI. You know, who to take and who to cut. We'll be back in less than an hour. You can leave for lunch right after I've checked your work."

I had managed to look stern during this exchange, but as soon as Chuck and I left the dome, I burst out laughing. Chuck joined me in that activity.

We took Chuck's red truck down to the town of Bella Villa, the seat of the county of the same name. It was an engaging little town. The main street contained a general store that stocked dry goods, sundries, and a small selection of groceries and meat; a second-hand store, which Chuck told me was really a pawn shop; a pet shop; a hardware store; a bar; and The Rabbit Hole Restaurant – our destination. The street also contained, of all things, a tattoo parlor. With the exception of the bar, every building boasted a fresh coat of paint. The contrast with No-Name was stunning.

Chuck pulled up in front of The Rabbit Hole. There were five red pickups and three red cars that I could see. I don't know how many more of them were around back. "What's with the red pickups?" I asked.

"I have n-n-no idea about the trucks," Chuck said. "The cars, though, are the coupe du jour."

We entered the restaurant and were waved to a table by a guy carrying a note pad and a pencil. "Hi, Chuck."

"Hello, Duane. How's your dog doing?"

"He'll survive, but I don't think he's gonna take on a raccoon again, any time soon. You want the usual?"

"For both of us. Bea, this is D-D-Duane. He's the owner, waiter, dishwasher, painter, and probably numbers runner for this place. Duane, meet Bea."

"Pleased to meetcha. Don't go believing everything Chuck says. He's a great kidder."

"Really?" I said. "I'm glad you told me. I was about to buy the Brooklyn Bridge from him."

Duane laughed a great deal harder than that remark deserved. He went off to get our orders, which turned out to be the famous Welsh rabbit and a glass of Bud. The rabbits had been topped by pearl tomatoes and shoved under the broiler. That was a good way to cook them.

"What's with the tattoo parlor?" I asked Chuck.

"It's an interesting story. The people who own the pawn shop also own the buildings on either side of their store – that's the pet shop and the tattoo parlor. They have t-t-tenants in those two places. The tenant that used to be where the tattoo parlor is now, a women's fashion store, went out of business. The pawn shop people, name of Burrows, had a hard time finding new tenants. Now, the Burrows are upstanding C-C-Christian folk and they weren't any too anxious to rent to the only nibble they got for that space – the tattoo parlor. So they struck a deal. The Burrows would come down in price but the tattoo parlor people, name of Wesley, had to promise not to tattoo anything blasphemous or otherwise evil like death's heads or d-d-dripping daggers or such. And that's written in the lease.

"Well, it turns out that Mr. and Mrs. Wesley used to be rough bikers..."

At that point Duane showed up at our table.

"You folks want anything else?"

"I'll have another beer, Duane. You want one, Bea?"

"No, thanks. I haven't finished this one."

Duane went to get Chuck's beer and Chuck resumed his story.

"So anyway, it turned out that the new tenants had recently got themselves born again and resolved to abandon their sinful ways and to take themselves to a new God-fearing place and never to tattoo anything

126

blasphemous or otherwise evil."

Duane came back with Chuck's beer. "You tellin' Bea about the Wesley's?"

"I am that."

"This ain't like most of Chuck's stories," Duane said. "This one is the Gods-honest truth." He left the beer and the check.

"So the upshot of the whole thing," Chuck finished, "is that Wesley got the parlor at a discount, the Burrows are still kicking themselves, and the whole town had a good laugh."

We drove back up the road to USAO. On the way, I asked Chuck when I might be able to do my participant-observer thing with Gomping.

Chuck pondered this. "I know I shouldn't be asking, but if there's no chance that Gomping will survive the transition, why bother? You already know that he doesn't do anything and for a p-p-place as small as USAO, the engineer doesn't need help."

"No, you shouldn't be asking. But I'll skip Gomping. There now, you didn't ask and I didn't tell."

"You know that I ran into Ben the other day?"

"I do."

"You know where we met?"

"I do."

"You okay with that?"

"I don't see that there's anything to be okay with or not okay with."

Chuck nodded and smiled.

We arrived at USAO, where Chuck went off to inspect Gomping's 'work' and I went to my office. Lorrie told me that a Congressperson had tracked me to the Observatory and wanted a call back.

Jim Daley could handle written communication with the Congress, and could probably handle the telephone. But Congressional staffers want to talk with someone senior or else they pouted.

I called the number and got a staffer. "Congressman McCool would like to visit LIT with a small group of constituents."

"Does he have a date when he would like to come?"

"October 30 in the afternoon."

"Is there anything in particular he would like to see?"

"Yes, he would like to visit the biology lab to satisfy his constituents that the animals are not being mistreated."

Animals. He wants animals. Maybe I could borrow an alpaca.

"I'm afraid we don't have a lab or any animals. I'm not sure who does. Maybe the National Institutes of Health. Unless he wants to go to the zoo."

"No animals?"

"No animals."

"Well, in that case maybe the Congressman won't want to visit. I'll check with him and let you know."

On that note, I left and returned to LIT.

Pie was still closeted with the OMB grill team. Don informed me that Freddie was not on the team. Nuts!

I checked my mail and phone calls, and did the rounds of my staff to assure myself of their well-being. By now it was time to go home, so I met Alex at the car and home we went, with a minor detour to get a few bags of apples.

Chapter 10

October 17, 1991

I pulled the car off the road at the alpaca farm. We retrieved the bags of apples and headed for the fence. The farmer was right. The critters were at the fence by the time we got the car doors closed.

The entire load of apples disappeared almost before they landed. One of the alpacas stuck its nose over the fence at the spot where I was standing. I kissed its nose. It nuzzled my nose. Maybe we should buy a farm. Alex looked at me and said, "No."

"No what?" I asked.

"No to what you're thinking. No farm."

"Yeah. I guess you're right. But it would be fun."

We returned to the car.

When I got to the office, I found a message from Freddie Langsteth asking me to call her. Freddie worked for OMB. She was on the grill team that oversaw the activities of LIT. Over the past several months, we had become friends. I called her.

"How come you weren't on the grill team this time?" I asked.

"The powers that be thought I was too close to you guys to be objective. They were afraid I'd give you soft balls to hit out of the park."

"Were they right?"

Freddie snickered. "They'd have been better off with me. Pie charmed the socks off the team that went."

"I take it that Pie did okay."

"Okay? If it were up to that team, they'd boot Bush out of the White House and install Pie. Since that's not going to happen, they settled for a recommendation to increase your budget a great deal more than the Department asked for."

"Do you think we'll get the increase?"

"That's up to Congress, but if I were a betting woman, I'd bet 'yes.' We chatted a bit longer and hung up.

I went to get Don and together we told Pie the good news.

The day was starting off just fine. Bathed in that golden euphoria, I set out for USAO.

All was quiet when I entered the main building. Suddenly, Gomping burst from his office wielding a bamboo flute and a ukulele. The man was beside himself.

"Do you know what they did?" he screamed at me.

"No."

"Oh, oh, oh. What they did is they abolithed my job. Can you imagine? I'm supposed to pack my things and go to the Pentagon. Can you imagine, abolithing my job. *My job*. What will Chuck do without me?"

"I guess he'll have to work much harder."

Gomping squinted at me. "Did you have anything to do with this?"

"Tristram, I do not work for the Army."

"Phmph!" he said, wheeled, and stalked to his office.

I went through the corridor and into the dome to see if anything was going on there. Nothing that I could see, but the slit was open. I climbed the stairs and stuck my head out far enough to see that the harness and its accouterments were there. Visible evidence that the workmen were somewhere around. The trip-hammer was making an unholy racket.

Suddenly, I received a sharp push and I found myself through the slit and teetering on the narrow catwalk. A hard object was pressed against my back. "Hands up!" Up they went.

Before I could think, the harness was clipped around me and I was pitched off the catwalk. And there I dangled precariously.

The situation was somewhat unnerving. Or more accurately, terrifying. Once my brain again began communicating with the rest of me, I tried to assess the situation. Was there any feature of the harness that might ameliorate my predicament? The back of the harness was attached to a chain which, in turn, was attached to the building. In front, a clip was attached to a metal loop on one side of the harness. One half of a belt and I dangled from the loop. The other part of the belt dangled from a similar loop on the other side of the harness. There were various other features of the harness – things like straps for your legs and back, shoulder straps, and back braces. None of which did me the slightest good as I hovered lopsidedly over the precipice. I squirmed around, trying to reach the other piece of the belt. If I could get attached to that, at least I wouldn't be lopsided.

"Now," said a familiar voice, "you promise to tell them not to abolith my job."

Gomping. Who, it became clear, was a flaming nutcake.

"I can't tell them anything, Tristram, while I'm suspended here."

"No, but you can promise."

"Okay. I promise."

I looked down. Bad move. I had told Chuck that I wasn't afraid of heights. But this was a different matter. There are heights and there are heights and I was petrified. Vertigo was also a factor.

"How do I know you'll keep your promise?"

"Because I'm a very honest person."

A sudden gust of wind added to my discomfort. Look, Mommy, I'm flying.

"Are you thure you're very honest?"

Another voice. Lorrie. "Drop that and put your hands up."

Tristram dropped whatever he was holding and raised his arms.

"Now turn around slowly and walk into the dome." Exeunt.

Yet another voice. Bobby. "Hang on, Bea."

"Hang on to what?"

"Me."

Bobby edged over to the chain, hauled me up, and grabbed me in a bear hug. Which continued until I regained my composure. I looked at the floor of the catwalk upon which lay an instrument.

"Bobby, I will forever be grateful to you. But if you tell *anyone* that I allowed myself to get held up by a halfwit with a bamboo flute, I will stick pins in your dummy."

Bobby gave me big kiss. Lorrie, whose head was sticking through the slit remarked, "That is unseemly behavior."

We all walked back down to the dome, through the corridor, and into the common room. Letitia was just coming out of her office.

"There you are, Bobby. What's going on?"

Bobby jumped onto the refectory table.

> The man was a mis'rable brute,
>
> He held up poor Bea with a flute,
>
> But Lorrie did save her
>
> Her pen did not waver
>
> That they are *all* nuts remains moot.

"Are you telling me," Letitia said, "that someone used a flute to hold up Bea and Lorrie held up that someone with a pen?"

"That's what he's telling you," I responded. "Gomping was that 'someone.'"

Letitia shook her head. "You realize, I hope, that it was rather quiet here before you arrived."

I had to acknowledge that I realized that. I also realized that Gomping was not in sight.

I asked Lorrie where he was.

"I told him to take his ukulele and get out. Being a well brought-up Christian lady, I did not tell him what he could do with his flute."

"So he's on his way to the Pentagon?"

"I have no idea. All I know and all I care about is that he's out of here."

Amen to that.

"What does his car look like?"

Lorrie said, "It's a little light blue Chevy. Why?"

"I think I'd better call Sheriff Sam. If that nutcake sees someone in an Army uniform, he'll probably run him over."

"You think he's dangerous because he threatened you with his flute?" Letitia asked.

"Yes," Bobby answered. "And slapped her into a harness and dangled her over the precipice."

"On due consideration," said Letitia, "you'd better call the sheriff."

At this point, Worley and Chuck, who had been out for an early lunch, ambled in. "Wassup?" Chuck asked.

"For a short time, it was Bea," Bobby said, "but she is now down."

Lorrie gave the two men the details, leaving out only the limerick.

"Good God!" said Worley.

"Well," said Chuck, "it's good to know that Gomping can do some work if he puts his little m-m-mind to it."

I called Sheriff Sam, who said he would have his deputies look out for Gomping's car and would let me know when they picked him up. I told him I'd be back at LIT in about thirty minutes and gave him Don's and my phone numbers.

Don was in his office going over budget numbers with Ben. "You're back early," Don remarked.

"If Gomping had his way, I'd be even earlier. I'd have flown."

"Let me guess," Ben said, "he flipped you the bird?"

"Not quite." I proceeded to tell them what happened.

"Does Pie know?" Don asked.

"Not even Alex knows yet. I thought I'd wait until I heard from Sheriff Sam. He's going to either call here or to my office. I'd like to be able to tell Alex and Pie that the nutcake is behind bars and no danger to anyone."

On cue, Don's phone rang. It was Sheriff Sam. "Hang on a minute, Sheriff. Bea is here and I'll put this on speaker."

The nub of Sam's narrative was that his deputies spotted Gomping's car outside The Rabbit Hole. They looked inside the restaurant and there he was. Apparently Gomping did not believe that he had done anything wrong; he was therefore enjoying a leisurely lunch. When he was replete, he walked out to his car where the deputies nabbed him.

Gomping was indignant. He was a law-abiding citizen and he was personally going to see that their jobs were abolished. He was now residing in a cell and threatening to abolish every job in sight, including those of the two homeless drunks in the next cell.

"Bea," Sam asked, "are you going to press charges?"

"Yes, unless Pie asks me not to. I think getting him into the criminal justice system is the only way he can get a psychiatric evaluation. He'd never agree to one if it was voluntary."

Sam concurred.

I called Pie to make sure he was free and then called Alex and asked him to meet us in Pie's office.

Once more I went through the description of my aerial experience.

"Genug! No more USAO for you. Stay here and write your report."

"But Pie," I said, "that makes no sense. The guy who had it in for me is in jail. There is no reason to believe that I'm in further danger."

"That's what you said last time. What makes you think he's going to stay in jail?" Pie asked.

"That's what I wanted to ask you. I'm inclined to press charges, so that he'll stay there at least until he has a psychiatric evaluation. Will that cause you problems?"

"No. It's a good idea. Okay. Spend a few more days there – but on the condition that the sheriff keeps that *meshuggina* locked up."

"It's a deal."

I put the phone on speaker and called Sheriff Sam. I told him that I would press charges, and asked him to keep Gomping on ice. He asked me to stop at his office to sign papers. Then he would set the wheels in motion to arrange the psychiatric evaluation and allow Gomping to call his lawyer. The lawyer would, no doubt, demand that Gomping be released. But it was highly unlikely that any judge would permit that unless the psychiatrist reported that someone who did what Gomping did was totally sane.

Following the phone call, our discussion revolved around the question of whether Gomping was responsible for the two murders. He was mightily annoyed with poor Wumpus, but we couldn't see what was his beef with Larry Pottle.

"Follow the money," Ben offered. So saith the exec officer.

Chapter 11

October 18, 1991

She flies through the air with the greatest of ease

Above the great dome and above the big trees

She could see all the rivers and six of the seas

But she still yearned to be on the ground

Alex pulled off the road. "Do you think the alpacas will like that song?"

We got out of the car and retrieved the apples for what we now regarded as the Alpaca Toll Booth.

The herd of toll takers greeted us at the fence. When the apples were gone – it took about 30 seconds – Alex threw back his head and repeated his song in a lusty tenor. The alpacas turned their backs and retreated to a far corner of their pasture.

"Ungrateful wretches," Alex growled as we got in the car.

When we arrived at LIT, we were greeted by a delegation of Alex's nutty crew. One of them was dressed as the Cookie Monster. He was intoning "Cooookie, Cooookie." Two more of them wore placards pleading, 'Will work for food.'

"Aha!" said my husband. "I wondered why you weren't working. Okay. I'll bring cookies on Monday."

At which the Cookie Monster removed his head and they all skipped merrily to the lab.

I went directly to the jalopy and headed to the sheriff's office, with no stop at my place. There was nothing new to report on the USAO front. Sheriff Sam informed me that his job had been abolished by Gomping and that he was thinking of going home and filling out the unemployment compensation forms. He agreed to stick around while I signed the papers that would hold Gomping.

"What I don't understand," Sam said, "is how come nobody noticed what a lunatic that man is. How long has he been working there?"

"I'm not sure, exactly. Several years anyway. But since he seldom showed up for work he was just tabbed as a harmless eccentric."

"So why didn't they fire him?" Sam paused to reflect. "Yeah. It's the same in the County. More paperwork than it was worth."

"You got it." I thanked Sam for his help and continued on to USAO.

The entire staff (minus Gomping and Burnside but including Letitia and Bobby) was waiting for me. I gave them the news about Gomping, telling them that he was in the Bella Villa hoosegow in case anyone wanted to visit. No one seemed inclined to so do.

Letitia remarked, "Any further report will be anticlimactic, but is there any other little thing you might want to tell us?"

"Well, yes. Lorrie and Call-me-Colonel are quite sure that Dr. Pottle was alone in the dome, but neither of them actually saw him after he went through the door. The written log confirms that he was alone. But when Worley and I went to the shed to continue my education, we inadvertently discovered that the relevant tape had been corrupted. It isn't clear how it got itself corrupted."

Worley said, "I'm sure it was Gomping. Chuck and I have talked about it and I think Chuck's right – it couldn't have happened just because Gomping brought some magnetic-tipped screwdrivers into the shed. But now that we know how crazy he is, he probably did it on purpose."

"But why?" I asked.

"Don't know," Chuck answered. "But if P-P-Pottle wasn't alone but woke up a sleeping Gomping, the might have been trying to keep anyone from knowing that he was asleep on the job."

"But why," I persisted, "would he have done something as drastic as killing Pottle?"

Lorrie stuck her two cents in. "The man is deranged. You saw what he did to you for no reason at all. Or else it was an accident. He might have been fooling around with the control box and accidentally knocked him off."

At this point, Bobby jumped up on the refectory table. Groans all around.

There once was a poor backup tape,

Discovered in very poor shape,

Its file corrupted

Its psyche disrupted

The tape was a victim of rape

No sooner had Bobby jumped off the table than the doorbell chimed, the door opened, and Call-me-Colonel stepped into the room.

"I'm back," he announced. "I take it that you missed me."

"Oh, certainly," Lorrie said, "Where were you?"

Call-me-Colonel frowned. "That is not a proper question to put to your superior. Did anything important happen in my absence?"

Chuck said, "Perhaps it would be b-b-better if I wrote a report. Oral reports tend to leave things out. Would you like it in t-t-triplicate?"

"Duplicate will do." Call-me-Colonel stalked to his office.

"Did anyone know he was gone or for how long?" I asked.

Head shakes.

"I'll bet he was with his popsie," Lorrie said.

From Bobby. "Do you think he'd know what to do with a popsie?"

From Lorrie. "It doesn't bear thinking about."

As the group broke up, Bobby touched my arm. "Join me in Letitia's office."

Letitia closed the door behind us and we gathered around the coffee table. Bobby pulled what looked like an oversized calculator from his pants pocket.

"This," he said, "is Hewlett Packard's new palmtop. It's a cross between a calculator and a computer. It's a great little gadget and it can communicate with small computers. So I was fooling around with it..."

Letitia put in, "Bobby has an undergraduate degree in electrical engineering. He'll tinker with anything electrical. I'm expecting him to make my floor lamp do the dishes."

"I'm working on it," Bobby said. "Anyhow, I started to wonder if the little HP could communicate with the Vax. So early one morning, I took the palmtop into the shed, connected the serial ports and dropped a short program into the Vax. The program told the Vax to copy to the palmtop any data as it arrived. Since the Vax didn't need supervision, I left the palmtop in the cabinet and departed. And being an obedient little Vax, it did what it was told."

"Bobby," said Letitia, "spare us the suspense. Do you have the missing data?"

"Coincidentally, I chose the day that Pottle fell to try my experiment, so the data should be there," Bobby said. "I just haven't gotten around to examining it closely. Let's look."

"If it's okay with you, Bobby, I'd rather not do that here. I'd hate to have someone walk in on us while you're trying to decode the data. I'm pretty sure Alex's lab can do the decoding. May I take the palmtop to him? He might be able to do it tonight and give us the results when we have dinner at Pie's tomorrow night."

That seemed like a good idea to both Bobby and Letitia.

I stopped by Chuck's office, where he and Worley were conspiring to write the report for Call-me-Colonel. I added my bit of bureaucratic prose. "Man," said Chuck, "just wait'll he finds out that Gomping's in the c-c-clink, you're pressing charges, and we made him wait for a report to learn about it."

"What do you mean *we* made him wait," Worley said, laughing. "My recollection of the conversation is that *you* made him wait."

"Well," Chuck huffed, "if you don't want to share the credit, you can't share the glory."

On that note, I left for LIT, the palmtop safely stowed in my slacks' pocket.

I went directly toward Alex's wing of LIT. I heard the tenor warbling of "The Modern Major General" emanating from his office. As I walked toward the sound, one of the techies – I think it was the Cookie Monster – stuck his head out of his office door. "Hey, Bea, can't you make him stop?"

"I'll give it a try, but no promises."

I entered Alex's office and he stopped in mid-warble. He grabbed me, gave me a healthy smooch, and said, "Aha, my dear, have you come to be ravished?"

"I'm amenable, but we'll have to put it off for another day."

I took Bobby's palmtop out of my pocket, handed it to Alex, and asked if it could be read.

"Sure. I'll get it done right now. Unfortunately, it won't take long enough for a serious ravishment."

He walked down the hall and gave the palmtop to one of the techies for deciphering. While we waited for the results I explained what Bobby had done.

Alex gave a little whistle. "Too bad he's an astronomer, I'd like him in my group."

It didn't take long for the techie to come back with the readout. The log revealed that the slit was open at the time Pottle was on the catwalk and the controls had been adjusted so that the dome would revolve, causing anyone on the catwalk to be shoved outward.

"Uh oh," said Alex.

"I didn't want it to be murder," I said.

We took the palmtop and the readout and went to find Don and Pie.

Don was nowhere to be found, but Pie was in his office, on the phone. He cut the conversation short and said, "So *nu*?"

He listened in silence as we told him.

"So any one of four people could have done it, no?"

Alex and I nodded.

"I think," said Pie, "that it's time to take Ben's advice and follow the money. Bea, do you know if the sheriff removed whats-his-name's records?"

"The exec officer? George Wumpus. I'm not sure, I can call Sam and find out."

"Do that, please. If he has them, ask him if you can borrow everything. If he is willing, pick them up on your way to USAO on Monday. If not, please get them from Wumpus's office. In either case, bring them back so that Ben can take a look. Alex, please accompany her. I don't want Bea alone with a possible murderer."

"Pie, if I call Sam right now we can find out if he's got the records."

"You're right. Call him from here."

I called. Sam had the records and we arranged to pick them up the next morning, Saturday.

Chapter 12

October 19, 1991

Saturday greeted us with an impenetrable fog. Alex, still in pajama bottoms, turned on the radio to get the weather report, while I rummaged in the closet for my housecoat. Eventually I found it, hanging between a hostess gown — now why would I have a hostess gown? — and a Redskins jacket – another mystery. Alex reported that the fog was supposed to burn off by noon. It was now 9am.

I put the coffee on, set the table, and padded out for the *Post*. The front page was a classic illustration of 'slow news day'. A Japanese evangelical proclaimed the United States would be destroyed and China would be enslaved. Clarence Thomas was sworn in as a Supreme Court Justice, and Anita Hill said she had no regrets. While I read trivia, Alex assembled the makings of pancakes and began some serious cooking.

"Aren't we supposed to pick stuff up from Sheriff Sam this morning?" Alex asked.

"Yeah, but I don't think it's such a hot idea to drive up there in this fog. I'll call and ask if it's okay to be there this afternoon, after the fog disperses."

It was okay with Sam, who had his hands full with morning fog-induced accidents.

"Well," said my mate, "what should we do in the meantime?"

Now that was a no-brainer if ever there was one.

We rolled back out of bed around 11:30. The fog was beginning to lift. We took a shower and began to greet the day anew. We were due at Pie's and Bessie's that evening. Bessie was a marvelous cook but she didn't do desserts. We therefore decided that Alex would stay home and make cookies, and I would drive up to get Wumpus's records. "Hmm," Alex mused, his head already filled with sugar plums, "if I make an extra batch and freeze half the dough, then I can bake it tomorrow and feed my crew on Monday. Whaddya think?"

"Pure genius." I kissed the back of his neck.

"Do you think it would be okay if you left an hour later?"

"No, it wouldn't be okay. We'd be late for Bessie's dinner."

"Rats!"

Remnants of the havoc wrought by the fog littered the roadside. A fender here, a bumper there, burned out flares everywhere. But, with the fog lifted and sun shining through the clouds, I had a smooth journey to Bella Villa. I arrived at the station to find a gaggle of exhausted deputies sprawled on every available chair. Joe, my guide and savior, got up. "Hey Bea, Sam is in his office." Joe walked with me to Sam's place. "So you think it was a homicide, huh?"

"Sure does look like that."

"We're grateful for the help you folk have given us. We're just a tiny rural outfit. We do traffic accidents, domestics, bar brawls, all that kind of stuff – and we do it real well. But in the twenty years I've been a deputy here, this is my first, whaddaya callit, intellectual murder. That pumpkin shoot's got us all scratching our heads."

I smiled at him. "I don't see that we've been all that much help so far."

Joe opened Sam's door. "Bea's here, Sam."

Sam got up. He looked every bit as beat as his deputies.

"Sam, for goodness sake! Why didn't you tell me to come tomorrow?"

Sam gave me a tired smile. "If you're gonna solve this thing for us, the least we can do is make it easier for you."

He picked up an accordion folder from his desktop and handed it to me. "Here are all his papers. We took his computer for good measure." It was sitting on the floor next to his desk.

Joe said, "I'll take it to your car, Bea."

I accompanied Joe to the car, made room in the trunk for the machine, thanked Joe, and took off down the road to urban Virginia.

We drove into Pie's driveway just ahead of Letitia. Pie greeted us as Bobby drove up. Pie was wearing a butcher's apron over his impeccable leisure clothes. Letitia was wearing a decorous calf-length suit. As usual, the rest of us looked as if we had chosen our wardrobes at a rummage sale. Ah well, we had other virtues.

Alex presented Pie with the cookie offering, which Pie gratefully accepted. Pie then herded us into the living room and seated us around a long, low cocktail table covered with bowls of nuts, raisins, and other dried fruit. He ascertained that none of us wanted drinks and told us to amuse ourselves while he and Bessie finished up in the kitchen.

Having decided that discussion of the USAO mess should be put off until after dinner, we proceeded to amuse ourselves by examining the living room. It was an eclectic arrangement of antiques (the sturdy kind), sink-into chairs, various artifacts from Bessie's adventures in every continent and major island in the world, and – peeking out from behind a bookcase— a skeleton. We were initially unsure if it was something Bessie had unearthed or a remnant of Pie's career as a micro-biologist. We finally decided it was a Bessie souvenir since we couldn't think of any use a microbiologist would have for a skeleton.

Pie's contributions to the decor were dozens of framed photos of microbiological glamour pics. My favorite was a closeup of *Purple nonsulfur bacterium Rhodobacter ferrooxidans*.

Our host returned to the living room bearing a platter of what he told us were tequenos – cheese sticks that are found all over South America. "So," he said, "when you finish the *nosh*, I'll usher you into the dining room and we'll serve you the rest of your dinner." He vanished once more.

The tequenos were sufficiently delicious that they were gone in a flash. Alex and Bobby had a small altercation over which of them would get the last one. They finally decided to settle it in civilized fashion and cut it in two. In the time-honored tradition, one of them did the dividing and the other had first pick. Letitia and I marveled at the ease with which mature, exceptionally well-educated males reverted to childhood. Pie had reentered the room in time to witness the Cutting of the Cheese Stick. "You may join is in the dining room," he said, "if you promise not to start a food fight."

The dinner was up to Bessie's usual standard. She served a boned leg of lamb which had been grilled over a fire pit and a ratatouille cooked in one of the Etruscan-style clay pots. Pie had baked a wonderful crusty baguette, which he served with a flourish.

Throughout dinner, conversation revolved around food and Bessie's upcoming trip to Peru. A couple of Peruvian archeologists had, through the use of ground-penetrating radar, located a likely site for archeological success. Some hand augering had been performed which confirmed that the site was promising. An analysis of the material retrieved convinced them that they were really on to something. They were doing more extensive augering and, if the site appeared to be living up to its promise, they'd want Bessie there before the excavation begins. Bessie thought she'd be in Peru within a month.

After dinner, we retired to the living room with coffee, Alex's cookies, and Bobby's disk. We brought Letitia, Bobby, and Bessie up to date on the results of the readout. "So it really was murder," said Bessie. "A bad business."

"If we assume a single murderer," Letitia put in, "then four people could have done it – Burnside, Gomping, Doolittle, and Hadaman."

"Do any of them have a motive for both murders?" Bessie asked.

"And do all of them have the opportunity to do both murders?" Bobby added.

"There's something I haven't done that may cast a little light on this," Pie said. "I called New South Wales to offer condolences about Pottle, but I didn't ask if they knew why he wanted to talk to Letitia. It didn't seem important then, but now that it looks like murder, I'd better get on the phone again.

" It's a little after 9pm here – what time is it in New South Wales?"

Bessie, the globe-trotting archeologist answered immediately. "A little after 11am there. We're on daylight time and they're on standard time. You should be able to get them now."

"*Mazel Tov.*" Pie gave Bessie a kiss. "You are a fount of required information."

Pie went off to make the phone call. We occupied ourselves with useless speculation until he returned some fifteen minutes later.

"Hold on to your hats," he said. "Burnside plagiarized Lazuli's work." Pie had reached the Director of the Australia Telescope National Facility, who gave him the whole story.

Larry Pottle was Morgan Lazuli's nephew. Shortly before Lazuli died, he mailed Pottle a copy of his notes. Pottle, on receiving them, recalled that he had seen, in a recent issue of *The Astronomical Journal*, an article that seemed to be based on a portion of that work. He looked it up and found the article signed by Lieutenant Colonel Burnside of USAO. He brought the article and the notes to the attention of the

Director. Since the very eminent Dr. Krackov was at USAO and since Pottle was going to be in Washington for a meeting, they decided that, before doing anything else, Pottle would talk it over with her. The Director suspected that Pottle was using this as an excuse to meet Letitia, but Pottle was a good guy and the Director decided to humor him. Now, of course, he wished he hadn't.

They were trying to figure out whom they should call to tell about the plagiarism – the Army brass or Letitia – when Pie called and took them off the hook.

"Geez! That certainly does shed some light on things," said Alex. "But Burnside isn't an astronomer. No way could he understand enough of the work in Dr. Lazuli's notes to get a paper out of them."

"According to the briefing book," I said, "Burnside has a Masters degree in physics/astronomy. He wouldn't be capable of doing that level of research, but he should be able to understand someone else's work."

"That explains it," said Alex. "Okay. Let's get organized."

Pie went to get pencil and paper and we constructed a Table.

Name	Marksman	Opportunity	Motive	
			Wumpus	Pottle
Burnside	?	Yes	?	Plagiarism revealed
Gomping	?	Yes	Vengeance	?

Doolittle	?	Yes	?	?
Hadaman	?	Yes	?	Afraid of being "outted"

"Well," remarked Letitia, "we do seem to have a surfeit of question marks."

"Maybe Ben can fill in some of them when he looks at the Wumpus files," Alex said.

Bobby got that faraway look in his eye.

Pie turned to me. "Is this what you meant?"

"Unfortunately, yes."

> We drew a beautiful table,
>
> Each cell had its own nice label,
>
> But we didn't know squat,
>
> Couldn't tell what was what,
>
> Right now the Table's a fable.

And on that depressing note, we thanked Bessie for her wonderful dinner and went to our respective homes.

Chapter 13

October 21, 1991

Alex and I stopped at our little grocery store and picked up four bags of apples. The clerk said, "I been noticing that you folks use an awful lot of apples. What do you do with 'em all?"

Alex said, "We feed them to the alpacas."

"Hmmph," said the clerk as he rang up the sale, "if you don't wanna tell me, then don't tell me."

"But..." said Alex. It was too late. The clerk had already turned his back on us and moved away.

We took our apples and left. I slid into the driver's seat, leaned over and gave my husband a peck on the cheek. "It's okay," I consoled him, "we can straighten the guy out next time."

The farmer came up to us as we paid our Alpaca Toll. "You folk really like them animals, don't you?"

We agreed that we did.

"Well, I got a little proposition for you. Now you don't wanna answer right away, but chew it over for a few days and then let me know if it sounds like something you'd like to do."

155

"We can't afford to buy the farm," Alex said.

The farmer laughed. "And I can't afford to sell it. Now here's the deal. I got a little log cabin on the property. It's got a bitty kitchen and a room with a fireplace and a small bedroom with a double bed. It's got electricity and uses propane for heat and cooking. For water, it's on the same well and septic as the main house. Has a window air conditioner. My son and his wife used to live there until they got enough money to buy their own place. The wife and I kinda miss having them around.

"So anyway, we thought if you two want to use the place for weekends or whatever, we could let you have it if you'd just pay the utility bills and keep the place up. Don't answer now – chew it over and if it sounds like something you'd like to do, let me know next time you're here and I'll show you the place."

With that, he turned and returned from whence he came.

Nonplussed, Alex and I looked at one another. "What do you think?" Alex asked.

"I don't know. Let's sleep on it and 'chew it over' in the morning."

Alex had baked the promised cookies. They were in two bags, a largish one for his crew and a smaller one for the admin folk. I went directly to Ben's office with the accordion folder full of the Wumpus files.

"His computer is in the car," I told Ben. "Do you think you'll need it?"

Ben shrugged. "Let's take a look at the paper first. That may be all I need."

"Come with me to Don's office and I'll tell you both the News of the Week."

Don had not yet been told of the hanky-panky with the housekeeping data, so I started from there, continued through Bobby's duplicate disk, and finally to Call-me-Colonel's thievery.

"Holy cats!" Don looked at Ben. "Not only did we miss the whole thing but we didn't even get one of Bessie's dinners."

"Just as well," Ben said, "since the Colonel's in the soup."

"That's the *lieutenant* Colonel," I corrected.

I bestowed a few cookies on him, and he went back to his office to begin inspecting the Wumpus file.

"Do you have a briefcase here?" I asked Don.

"Sure, why?"

"Put the cookies in it so we can smuggle them past Lenore. She's supposed to be on a diet. We shouldn't tempt her."

Virtuously, we tucked the cookies away and sauntered off to Pie's office.

Pie was on the phone with the director of the Human Resources department. He finished the conversation and hung up. "Why did they change the name from 'Personnel Department'? 'Human Resources' sounds like a slave labor camp."

"I suppose," said Don, "that some places would regard that as an accurate description. What's up with them?"

"The head of our Facilities Management group is retiring. We're going to have to start advertising the job."

This was not a trivial matter. In the normal course of events, we would first decide whether we would limit the advertisement to the department (DoTI), to the entire government, or would let it go out to the country at large. After thirty days, the Office of Personnel Management (OPM) — now why isn't it the Office of Human Resources? — scores all of the responses, taking into consideration not just the qualifications, but whether the candidate is a veteran, a member of an official minority, disabled, and heaven knows what else. Then they take the top three scorers and send them to the place-in-need to pick one. If that place doesn't like any of them, OPM sends over the next three.

"I do not need to deal with this *mishegas* now."

"You may not have to," I said. "That's one of the reasons I wanted to talk with you before I go to USAO."

At that point, Don offered the bag of cookies to Pie, who helped himself. He looked at Don's briefcase. "So that's how you sneaked them past Lenore?"

"She's on a diet," Don and I said in unison.

"That's considerate of you. So tell me what you wanted to talk with me about."

"I'm about ready to write my report on USAO. Chuck Hadaman doesn't have nearly enough to do. Aside from babying the telescope, he is the chief cook and bottle washer in the machine shop, and takes care of the facility. I was going to recommend that he add some duties at LIT in addition to what he does at USAO, but he'd be perfectly capable of heading up our Facilities group."

"From your description, it sounds like he has plenty to do," Don said.

"If you don't take into consideration the fact that the whole outfit has only about six people in it."

"And if," added Pie, "you don't take into consideration the possibility that he's a multiple murderer."

"Well, yes there is that. Do you want me to hold off on the report and hang around USAO until we catch the bad guy?"

"No," Pie said. "Better write the report. We can sit on it until there's some resolution. The current head of Facilities isn't going to leave for another three months, so we have time. Would Hadaman have to answer an advertisement?"

"No. Once the transfer is complete, he belongs to DoTI. They just put him in for a promotion and slide him into the merged Facilities position. If it looks like there might be objections, we can assign him the duties without the title and then take care of that later."

"When do you think DoTI will take over?" Don asked.

"Soon, I think. As you know they've already abolished Gomping's position, so the Army is on the move."

"How about Hadaman? Will he go for it?" Pie wondered.

"I think so. If it's okay with you, I want to talk with him about it today."

"Get Alex to go with you," Pie directed. "You need an escort if you're going to meet with a possible murderer."

"Before you go," Don asked, "have you had your flu shot?"

"Not yet, why?"

"The flu season's starting early this year. The Beijing flu has already closed some schools in Ohio. It takes about two weeks for the shots to be effective, so I'm going to the nurse's office to get a shot. Hopefully, it'll take effect before the flu gets here. You and Alex should get shots too."

Pie said he would accompany Don to the nurse's office. I called Alex and gave him the double good news. First a flu shot and then USAO. Pie and Don were leaving the nurse's office as Alex and I walked in.

The door chimes announced us and Lorrie met us at the door.

"Boy, am I glad to see you guys. We're rattling around in here. Wumpus is dead and gone, Gomping is just gone, and Worley called in with the flu. He's gonna miss his elliptical galaxy meeting and probably Bad Movie Night. It's a shame."

"We just got our flu shots. Have you had yours?"

"Not yet. I'll get one on the way home."

"Is Chuck in?" I asked.

"He's in his office."

Call-me-Colonel stuck his head into the common room, saw that it was just me and someone who didn't look important, and pulled his head back in.

I banged on Chuck's door.

"Yo."

"This is my husband, Alex Carfil. Alex, meet Chuck Hadaman."

"What b-b-brings you here?" Chuck asked.

"I'm about to write my recommendations to DoTI and I wanted to talk with you about it."

Chuck looked quizzically at Alex, but receiving no explanation, said, "Let's go into the small conference room where there's room for the three of us to s-s-sit down."

We repaired to the conference room and sat.

I explained the plan to bring Chuck into the LIT fold as head of Facilities. "Would that appeal to you?"

"Damn straight! But have you taken into c-c-consideration that I may be a murderer?" He looked at Alex. "Aha. You're her bodyguard."

Alex grinned. "That's me. But since you're twice my size..."

"Yes," I cut in. "I have taken that into consideration. If it turns out that you're of murderous bent, I'll rescind the recommendation."

Chuck laughed. "Then go for it."

We knocked on Letitia's door, intending to pay our respects and depart USAO. Bobby was in her office. Letitia said, "Sit down. We have a question for the management scientist."

We sat. Bobby said, "Here's the problem. Letitia has all Morgan Lazuli's notes. There's significant work there, and I'd like to expand on those notes, develop some papers, maybe even a book, and publish with appropriate attribution to Dr. Lazuli. What he's done is a lot more interesting — and a lot more important — than the research I'm doing right now."

"So what's the problem?" Alex asked.

"It's a question of ownership," I answered. "Dr. Lazuli was ailing – I think he had lung cancer — and at the tail end of his career. The Army set him up here, similar to the arrangement with Letitia. The difference is that he was an actual employee of the Army. Therefore, the Army might claim that the rights to the notes belong to the Army. They'd have a good case."

"So what should we do?" Letitia asked.

"Normally," I said, "Bobby would go to the Commanding Officer and ask permission to use the notes. But since the Commanding Officer is Call-me-Colonel...."

"Oy," said Letitia.

"Not to worry. Pie can go over Burnside's head to his superior, probably a full colonel, and ask for that permission. Because Bobby isn't a Federal employee, I don't believe he would have to go through all the rigamarole required to get permission to publish. He only needs permission to use the notes. My guess is that the colonel will check with a Judge Advocate General, who most likely will agree with me. Then the colonel will grant permission with the proviso that any publication resulting from use of the notes gives appropriate credit to the Army. Pie can be pretty persuasive."

Letitia thought for bit. "Can you set that in motion soon?"

"Assuming Pie is available, as soon as we get back to LIT."

"But before we go, maybe you can answer something that's been bothering both Alex and me."

"I'll try. What is it?"

"Everyone agrees that Dr. Lazuli was reclusive and didn't publish. And everyone agrees that he was eminent. But if he didn't publish, how did anyone know that his work was worth diddley squat?"

Letitia said, "Every once in a while you get someone like that. Someone who disapproves of publishing. They won't tell you why. The silliest reason I've heard is that one reluctant author didn't want to cut down so many trees. I can understand this if the person's work is garbage – he wouldn't want it submitted for peer review. But someone like Lazuli is a complete mystery to me.

"He published just enough to get tenure at RPI, but once he had tenure he refused to publish again. So he never made the jump from associate to full professor. His students adored him. He was the PhD advisor to a number of astronomers who have become very well known. And more than that, he deigned to teach undergraduates. I don't know how many of those kids became astronomers because of him.

"So between the PhDs and the undergrads, he became known as a first-rate teacher and astronomer. When he retired from RPI – I think because his health started to go – he got a research associate position here. I believe one of his undergrads, who later became a big wheel at the Pentagon, arranged it for him. I think he was supposed to be pulling his notes together for a book. But that was never going to happen. Bobby is the best hope for that."

Alex and I got up.

"Amazing bio," said Alex. "Thanks for telling us."

"One more question," I said. "What's with the limericks, Bobby? You're a serious scholar, why play the clown?"

Letitia smiled. "Sit back down."

We sat.

Bobby said, "When I was still an undergraduate, we would-be astronomers had to take a course given by an associate professor who was one of the nastiest entities ever to pretend to be a human being. He ridiculed everything we said or wrote. A lot of us were seriously considering changing our major. I didn't have any such thought. I just regarded the class as a rite of passage, gritted my teeth, and soldiered on. But I was worried about my classmates.

"I always had a knack for writing limericks so I wrote a nasty limerick about the man and told my fellow-sufferers to meet me at the Union after class. We commandeered a big table and I jumped up on a chair and presented my limerick."

Letitia then took up the narrative. "The kids clamored for more. Bobby promised them a new one after each class but those who dropped the class would not be welcome at the table. And so it was that all those who signed up for the class saw it through to the end – the first time that ever happened.

"Well, when Bobby arrived here he saw a similar situation with Call-me-Colonel and those who labored under him. So for that similar situation, he tried a similar solution. And the rest is history.

"You may leave now."

Alex and I departed, satisfied.

As we left, Lorrie called after us, "Don't forget Bad Movie Night on Wednesday."

No way would we forget.

We got in the car and started back to LIT.

"How did Burnside get hold of Lazuli's notes in the first place?" Alex wondered.

"Easy. Except for Burnside's sanctum, all of the offices have the same keys. Burnside only had to come in one night, go into Lazuli's office, run the notes through the Xerox machine, and put them back where he found them. In addition to the time it would take to get permission to publish, it can take a year or more to get a paper into *The Astronomical Journal*. Sick as Lazuli was, it was good bet that he'd be dead before *The Journal* came out. Or if not dead, too weak to read it."

We arrived at LIT, and Alex went back to his lab. I stopped in Ben's office.

"Anything?"

"I think so," said Ben. "Give me until tomorrow morning and I'll wrap it up in a ribbon and bow for you."

I agreed. I went off to find Pie who, I discovered, had been summoned to the Department. He wouldn't be back that day.

So I trudged to my office and dealt with all the stuff I was paid to deal with.

Tomorrow promised to be interesting.

Chapter 14

October 22, 1991

We stopped at the grocery store to pick up our alpaca offering. The clerk ignored us as best he could. Alex put the apples on the counter and went over to propitiate the clerk. "These really are for alpacas," he said.

"Sure they are," the clerk muttered.

"No, really, there's an alpaca farm on our way to work and we stop to feed them. They're cute critters."

"No shit?" asked the clerk.

"No shit," said Alex.

"Are they anything like llamas?" the clerk asked.

"They're related, but llamas are big – they can go over four hundred pounds. The alpacas are about a hundred, hundred and fifty at most."

"By the way, I'm Alex."

"I'm Buddy." They shook hands.

I walked over. "This is my wife, Bea." More handshakes.

"You know," Buddy said, "we're real particular about our apples here. We inspect 'em every morning and if one looks like it's starting to get brown, we yank it. You want I should save those for you? The alpacas'll like 'em just the same and you won't have to buy so many."

We accepted the offer with alacrity, paid for our bags of Inspected and Certified Good apples, loaded them in the backseat, and headed up the road.

It was Alex's turn to drive, and therefore my turn to nibble on an ear. "Hey," Alex cried, "you shameless hussy!" He pulled off the road, unbuckled his seat belt, and grabbed me. We were just settling in for a satisfying snoggle, when a tap on the window caught our attention.

A trooper. The same trooper who had interrupted us before. Alex lowered the window. "Geez," said the trooper, I should have recognized the car. It's you two crackpots again."

Alex reached into the backseat and retrieved a piece of fruit. "Would you like an apple?" he asked.

The trooper started to return to his cruiser, thought better of it, turned back, took the apple, and went on his way.

We did the same, stopping only at the Alpaca Toll Booth to deposit our tribute. The farmer did not appear. He was giving us time to 'chew things over.'"

I hotfooted it to Ben's office. "What have you found?"

"Skullduggery. Should I give it to you now or should we let Don and Pie in at the start?"

"Don and Pie."

We collected Don, wove around Lenore's desk, and interrupted Pie up to his elbows in paperwork.

"*Nu?*"

"Ben followed the money and hit the jackpot," I said. "It's your show, Ben."

It was a travel fiddle. Worley was authorized to attend a week-long meeting in California. He flew round trip economy class to San Francisco, rented a car to get to Berkeley, and booked into an inexpensive hotel. The return trip was equally innocuous. The time in between was another matter. According to Wumpus's notes, he, Wumpus, received a call from someone on the meeting's administrative staff. There had been a fire in the kitchen of the place where they had intended to hold the keynote banquet. The venue had therefore been moved. They had managed to contact all of the attendees with the exception of Worley Doolittle. No one at the meeting remembered seeing him. He had paid for his room, but on checking, the hotel staff reported that his bed had not been slept in. Could USAO try to locate him and give him the new banquet location? Wumpus said he would try.

Wumpus then went to his files and discovered that Doolittle often traveled to meetings in California but seldom anyplace else. Apparently Worley had been taking California vacations at USAO's expense. There was no way of knowing if Worley had been confronted before Wumpus's untimely demise.

Don gave a low whistle. "Now what do we do?"

"This is not evidence that Doolittle killed Wumpus," Pie said. "It gives him a motive, but only if he had already been confronted. So – the most we can do is fill in a cell in our Table, not an earthshaking event, and present the travel fiddle to DoTI. It's up to the Department to either hand the hot potato to the Army or to wait for the transfer and act on the information then."

He turned to Ben. "You did a good job. Thanks."

"Pie," I said, "I think Sheriff Sam would appreciate it if we brought him up to date. If he's available, we can stop in Bella Villa on the way home."

"Good idea."

"Bea," Ben said, "is Wumpus's computer still in your car?. If you're going to Bella Villa you can drop it off."

Pie asked, "Have you been *shleping* that thing all over Maryland, Bea?"

"It was not being *shlepped*. It was riding in comfort in the trunk. I'll drop it off."

With that we adjourned to the cafeteria. During lunch, we desultorily talked of cabbages and kings.

After lunch, Don and Ben toddled back to their respective offices. Pie and I stopped at my place.

"You got something else on your mind?"

I explained Bobby's problem. "His first step would normally be to get permission from the Commanding Officer to use Lazuli's notes, but since the Commanding Officer is..."

"Burnside," Pie said, "I see the problem. How can I help?"

"Could you call Burnside's superior and start the process from there?"

Pie didn't even stop to think. "With pleasure. I'd like to help the kid any way I can. I'll start things rolling right now."

He hit the intercom button. "Lenore," he said, "Lieutenant Colonel Burnside is the commanding officer at USAO. Without calling USAO, please find out the name and phone number of his superior officer."

"Certainly, Dr. Pie."

Pie disconnected. "Lenore is an absolute genius at getting information. She's wasted here. She should be at CIA."

I left Pie's office with the absolute certainty that things were in good hands.

I stopped in my office, took care of urgent matters, and updated my copy of the Table. Then I called Alex and asked him to meet me at the car in ten minutes. That would give me time to Xerox Ben's report.

"Boy, will I be glad when this USAO crud is over," Alex grumbled. "I'm not getting much work done here."

"You and me both," said I.

Alex strolled up to the car just as the micro-managing Ben was ensuring that the computer was, in fact, in the trunk. "That was really a nice job you did," Alex told Ben. "I'm not sure it would have occurred to us to follow the money."

"Then," Ben remarked, "you would have remained clueless."

We drove up to the Sheriff's office, and Alex began to unload the computer. Joe intercepted him. "I'll get that."

Joe, the computer, Alex, and I entered the building. "Is Sam in?"

"In his office," Joe said. "You got something for him?"

"Not a solution," I answered, "but something."

Joe took the computer to the evidence room. Alex knocked on Sam's door, and we were welcomed into the office.

I handed Sam the updated Table.

Name	Marksman	Opportunity	Motive	
			Wumpus	Pottle
Burnside	?	Yes	?	Plagiarism revealed
Gomping	?	Yes	Vengeance	?
Doolittle	?	Yes	Travel fiddle	?
Hadaman	?	Yes	?	Afraid of being "outted"

I also turned over the copy of Ben's notes. Then we went through the Table cell by cell.

"Man, you guys are really on top of this. I can't tell you how much we appreciate it. If you ever get stopped by a cop, let me know and I'll fix it."

Alex and I burst out laughing.

"What's so funny?"

We told him about the times our snoggles were interrupted by a representative of the State.

Sam also thought it was funny.

We left Sam's place and got in the car to finish our drive home. "You know," Alex pointed out, "by the time we're halfway home, every deputy in the County will know the details of our encounters with the State trooper."

I put my head in my hands. "Oh, God."

Chapter 15

October 23, 1991

What with one thing and another, Alex and I hadn't managed to chew over the farmer's offer of the cabin in exchange for utility payments and upkeep. We began chewing that along with our pancakes.

"I don't see what harm it would do to take a look at the cabin," Alex said.

"The only thing that's bothering me," I replied, "is that it sounds too good to be true. And when something sounds too good to be true..."

"...it usually is," Alex finished. "But we can still look at the place and if there's a hooker, we don't have to take it."

That decided, we did the dishes and set off for the grocery store. A fine drizzle necessitated the windshield wipers.

Buddy was awaiting us with three bags of only slightly brown apples. "You only have to buy one bag today," he announced.

We thanked Buddy and ponied up for the single bag.

"Oh," I said, "We forgot popcorn. Do you have popcorn?"

"Yep. You want it in the raw or already popped."

Alex and I consulted and settled on popped. We bought a lot of it.

"I was wondering," Buddy said, "if I could follow you up the road one of these days so I could have a look at the critters. You got me all curious."

"Sure," I said.

"When's your day off?" asked Alex.

"Well, now that's a puzzler," Buddy replied. "I don't really have a day off. If I want to go someplace or something, I just ask Dad if he'll switch his time with mine. I generally work the mornings and he works the afternoons. Sunday we're closed, but you don't go up there on Sunday."

"Oh," I said, "this is a family-run business."

"It is. My mom used to take the morning shift. I was in high school then and played a little ball after school, so I wasn't working here. But then my mom died about five years ago and I stepped in. It's a good job and Dad and I enjoy talking to folks. Safeway took some of our business when they moved in, but most of the customers came back."

"Why'd they come back?" Alex asked.

"Well, the company line is that we have better stuff than the super-market but if you wanna know the truth, I don't think that's true for most things. I think in this area there are a lot of what I call reverse snobs. They like to shop here because think they're supporting us poor, uneducated ninnies who'd be driven to unemployment comp without them."

"And would you be?" I asked.

"Hell no. If worse came to worst we'd go work in the supermarket. Probably make more money, too. But it wouldn't be as much fun."

Alex and I laughed. "Well, let us know when you've made your arrangements with your dad and we'll lead you up there."

While Alex loaded the apples and popcorn into the back, I slid into the driver's seat and started the car. We mulled over Buddy's exposition on the way up the road.

"Do you think we're reverse snobs?" I asked.

"No," said Alex. "We shop there because they sell apples by the bag."

"Good," I said. "I wouldn't like to be a reverse snob."

The just-started-to-turn-brown apples filled the car with a distinct *eau de* apple perfume. "Next time, maybe we should put the apples in the trunk."

Alex agreed.

We were tossing the apples over the fence when the farmer appeared. "I don't believe," he said "that I ever told you my name. I'm Daryl Coker." He held out his hand. Alex shook it. "I'm Alex Carfil and my wife's Bea Goode."

I got the look. "I can't help it," I said. "My parents just weren't thinking when they named me."

The farmer considered this. "Well, I suppose 'Bea Carfil's' not much better. Would you like to look at the cabin now?"

"We would."

"Best take the car up, it'll be easier to get on your way when we've finished."

Daryl got in back, next to the popcorn, and directed us up the road past the alpaca's pasture and then onto a narrow gravel road to the house. A barn was just past the house. A plump gray-haired woman in blue jeans and a flannel shirt came out to greet us. "I'm Daryl's wife, Claudia." The handshake ritual was repeated.

"Would you like to come in for a cuppa before you see the cabin?"

"Thanks, we'd love to, but we're going to be late for work as it is."

"Next time, then," said Claudia.

The farm was small for a Maryland farm, which averages about 150 acres. The Coker farm looked to me to be about 20 acres. Which was not surprising because alpacas don't take up much room. If you had cows, you would need an acre for each cow and her calf. Daryl told us that you can get as many as nine alpacas on an acre but five would be more comfortable. So if you allow for the house, barn, other outbuildings, and a generous kitchen garden, there was more than enough room for a herd of forty critters.

The four of us walked through the drizzle to the cabin, which was about 300 feet the other side of the barn. It had been gussied up a bit with freshly painted trim. A flagstone path started from nowhere in particular and stopped at a single step up to the door. An herb garden graced the left side of the building. I think a perennial garden was on the right side. Leaves of Lenten roses added greenery, but in October it was impossible to tell what else would come up in the spring.

Claudia ushered us into the living room. The first thing that we noticed was that the cabin was warm. Good.

The furniture was sturdy and comfortable. My expectation of wall-to-wall chintz was not met – the decor was serviceable and pleasant; the walls, which had not been plastered over, were well-caulked logs. There was a fireplace with wood stacked neatly to the side. Daryl said that further wood was the tenant's responsibility.

The kitchen consisted of a small sink, a two-burner stove, an under-the-counter dishwasher topped by a Formica counter, and a table for two. Minimal shelf space hung from the log wall.

The bedroom held a double bed and night stand. "The tenant is responsible for the linens," Claudia said. "The cover is on us." The cover was made of — what else — woven alpaca fiber. The bathroom off the bedroom had a commode, a sink, and a tiled shower. Not top of the line, but not bottom-of-the-line either.

All in all, it was a great place.

The four of us walked back toward the car. "What do you think," Daryl asked.

"Can we give you an answer tomorrow?" Alex answered. "Our only reservation is that we might not use it enough."

"Sure thing," said Daryl. He took a little spiral notebook from his barn coat pocket, wrote his telephone number, tore off the sheet, and gave it to Alex.

We waved so-long and took off for LIT.

Alex and I agreed that we loved the place. We also agreed that we should call Sheriff Sam and see if he knew anything about our would-be landlords.

When we got to LIT, I went to my office to call Sam. Alex went to his lab in the hope that he could get some work done.

I got Sam on the phone. "Do you know the Cokers?" I asked. "The people who have the alpaca farm."

Sam started laughing.

"What's funny?"

"Last week, Daryl took down your license plate number and asked me to do a background check on you. Once I found out who owned the car, I called him back and told him he didn't need a background check. I knew you and would vouch for your trustworthiness." He chuckled. "I lie a lot.

"You don't need a check on the Cokers, either. I've known them all my life. Went to school with Daryl Junior. Was an usher at his wedding. They're good folk. They don't like the cabin standing empty. Are you thinking of taking it?"

"I think so. It'd be fun having a week-end place."

"Good," said Sam. "You'll like the Cokers. They'll be friendly but they won't get in your face."

I thanked Sam and went off to disturb Alex.

He was in a meeting with his group, so I waited in his office until they broke up.

"D'ja call Sam?"

I told him of Sam's endorsement and we high five'd. Alex said he'd call Daryl in the morning and make the appropriate arrangements. Then we both settled down to get some work done.

I don't know about Alex, but I worked right through lunch, touching base with my Congressional contacts, responding to students and would-be post-docs, visiting Ethel and urging her to further efforts on her library tasks, and various other trivial tasks that I was overpaid to do. Congressman McCool's staffer called to say that, on second thought, the Congressman would take his constituents to the zoo.

Ethel chased me down as I was moving from triviality to triviality.

"Can you spare a minute, Bea?'

What now? I thought. "Sure."

We returned to her office and sat down. "I need an assistant," Ethel said. "This library task is a lot of work."

"There's no time limit on it," I responded. "Just do what you can each day."

"But I don't have time to do anything else."

Since Ethel got all of her assignments from me, I thought back on what else she had to do. I came up dry. "What else do you have to do?"

"Well, for one thing there's organizing the softball team."

I stood up. "Okay. You are hereby relieved from organizing a softball team or any other duty that I have not specifically assigned to you." I turned to leave.

"Be advised," Ethel said, "that I am prepared to file a Prohibited Personnel Practice grievance."

"Be my guest."

I called Don and Pie and told them that we were going to have to do something drastic about Ethel. I brought them quickly up to date – cupcake caper and all.

"If she's going to file a grievance, we may as well give her something to file about. I want to fire her."

Pie thought for a moment. "Can you take care of it?"

"Yes."

"Then go ahead. I'll back whatever you do."

I called Jim, Jeanne, and Marge and told them to meet me in the admin conference room right away. Once assembled, I told them that I was going to fire Ethel. As one, they applauded.

Then I explained about the grievance procedure. "She'll certainly file one on the grounds that we're retaliating because of that stupid nepotism grievance she filed."

"But," objected Jeanne, "that was just a nuisance filing."

"Yeah," Jim said, "But she could win it anyway. Lots of times when people think they're going to be fired they file a preemptive grievance, so their boss will be afraid of a retaliation suit."

I nodded. "That's right. And I don't want to let her get away with it."

"What do you want us to do?" Jeanne asked.

"She's been assigned, at one time or another, to each of you. And each time you've had her she's done something outrageous. Please document whatever it was that she did and, if you can manage it, put it on my desk before you leave."

"It will," said Marge, "be a pleasure."

By 4:30 I had my documentation.

From Jim: He had put Ethel in charge of school groups. She took a call from a teacher who had a class of mentally disabled students. The teacher would like to bring her students to LIT if we had someone who could explain what we did in terms that they could understand. Ethel told her that we had better things to do than hold the hands of a bunch of retards. Jim had received many calls about that. He sent Ethel back to me.

From Jeanne: Ethel was making travel reservations. One of the LIT staff asked for kosher meals on his flight to California. Ethel did not apprise the airline of the request and the traveler thus subsisted on crackers until he reached his destination. When Jeanne asked Ethel what had happened, she responded that if "those people" wanted special menus, they should bring their own food. Jeanne sent Ethel back to me.

From Marge: Ethel's assignment was to redact a paper written by two of our biologists. The paper had been pronounced excellent by their department head. Ethel gave the paper a full rewrite and when the authors complained that the meaning of the paper had been changed and the science in it was now incorrect, Ethel told them that she was the editor and that her version of the paper would be the one published. The authors complained to Dr. Goode who removed the paper from Ethel's jurisdiction. Marge sent Ethel back to me.

Well, I thought, that should do it.

About 5:30, Alex walked into my office and I realized that I was famished. Not so famished that I couldn't spare the time for a serious snoggle, but famished none the less.

"Unless we want to subsist on popcorn," Alex said, we ought to get something to eat."

"How about The Rabbit Hole?"

Chuck was sitting solo when we walked in. "Come join us," Alex invited.

"Don't m-m-mind if I do." Chuck moved his dinner to a larger table and we all sat.

Duane came over with Welsh rabbits for Alex and me. "You guys want beer?" We allowed as how we did.

I noticed two men sitting at the next table. It took me a few minutes to recall why they looked familiar. They were a couple of lawyers who solicited injury-related cases. They advertised on TV. Once they got a case, it didn't matter to them if they won it or not. They got paid in either event. In a word, sleazebags. In one of their recent ads, they had informed the public that they were hiring.

Was the solution to the Ethel problem sitting in this very room? I whispered my find to Alex. He said to Chuck, "I'm going to wash my hands."

Alex stood up. I kicked Chuck's ankle and discreetly beckoned him to follow Alex. They came back clean and informed.

I said to Chuck, "I'm afraid we might lose Ethel."

"How c-c-come?" he said. "I thought she was one of your best employees. You were planning to promote her."

"OPM turned it down. Said the position description didn't merit a raise in grade. It's hard to keep good employees happy with know-nothings like that in charge."

Alex shook his head. "Someone's gonna snap Ethel Goodfoot up in a wink. She told one of my guys that she was only staying at LIT if she got her promotion. If not, she was outta here. What is she – a GS-11?"

"Yeah. She's making a little over forty thousand."

"Too bad," said Alex. "She's worth a lot more than that."

The two sleazebags paid their bill and left.

Duane, who had been listening to the conversation, came over. "Trying to get rid of someone, huh?"

"Why Duane, whatever made you think that?" Chuck said.

"Oh, I dunno. Something just come over me." Duane started back to the kitchen. "Serve those two slickers right. They don't tip worth a damn." He continued on his way, laughing.

"Well," I said to Chuck, "now that we've set those wheels in motion, tell us about Bad Movie Night."

"I can't tell you much t-t-that you don't already know. It's usually just for astronomers, but since we're the host, Lorrie, me, and you are there on sufferance. I've never been to one before. I think almost everyone gets there around 7:00 and socializes for a while eating popcorn and then the movie starts around 7:30 or 8:00."

"Too bad Worley can't make it," Alex said.

Chuck nodded. "I'm not sure how big an audience we'll g-g-get. This flu season looks like it's gonna be a doozy."

Alex and I took turns telling Chuck about the cabin at the alpaca farm. "When do you think you'll take p-p-possession?"

I said, "Given the late hour that we're leaving after the show, we'd like to do it tonight..."

"Hey," Alex cut in, "we're gonna be late if we don't move it."

We paid our tabs and headed to USAO.

We rescued the bags of popcorn from the back and carried them to the propped-open door of the building. We distributed the bags around the room. The common room was already filled with a bunch of guys and a sprinkling of women – Letitia among them. She introduced us to Dr. Smathers, a small, not-quite-elderly man and explained to him my relationship with USAO.

"What in the world does DoTI want with a telescope?" he asked.

"They would like to examine asteroids to see if any useful minerals reside there."

"Hunh, seems like Doolittle has himself a fine berth. I wouldn't mind retiring into something like that myself."

"Except that Doolittle didn't officially retire into it," Letitia said. "He thinks it's a job."

"Well, whatever it is," Smathers said, "it would suit me just fine. At my advanced age, I think I've done as much serious work as I'm capable of. And I think examining asteroids for minerals would be interesting. If something else like that pops up, please think of me."

One of the multitude joined us. "Who just spread those bags of pop-corn around?"

"Why?" Alex asked.

"They taste like apples. Where'd you get them?"

"It's our own secret recipe," Alex said. "We thought this crowd might enjoy it."

The man looked at Alex skeptically, then shrugged and walked away. We wandered into the crowd.

Another man approached. "I don't recall seeing you people before. Do you work at USAO?" he asked Alex.

"Uh uh." Alex shook his head. "I'm Alex, the spouse. My wife, Bea, is helping with the transition to DoTI."

"Pleased to meet you both. I'm James." He reached over, grabbed a handful and stuffed the popcorn in his mouth. "Mmmmph glffle?" he continued.

"Huh?" Alex asked.

James swallowed. "Doolittle not here?"

"He has the flu," I said.

"I don't think he's made any of these things," James said. "He's a puzzle. We were all surprised he didn't have a brilliant career."

"I think his brother's death knocked him for a loop."

"Could be. I think they were pretty close – they were born about a year apart. The younger guy was just kind of ordinary. Worked as a salesman or something like that. Then he got accused of rape..."

"*What?*"

"Yeah. He hadn't been incarcerated yet. He was out on bail while they were still investigating the charges, so he went to talk it over with his big brother Worley. They were backpacking in the outback when the younger guy – I think his name was Wally – keeled over with a heart attack."

"Geez," Alex said, "that would be enough to knock anyone for a loop."

At that point, there was a general banging on the refectory table. "Ten minutes to movie time," Lorrie announced.

They had set up in front of the door to the corridor, placing the projector a few feet in front of the entrance door. Chairs – I wonder where they got them — were arranged and everyone sat down.

The door to the corridor opened and Call-me-Colonel squeezed past the screen. "I would like to welcome you," he blathered and gave some kind of speech. The audience took the opportunity to chat with the people around them. Call-me-Colonel vanished behind the screen, and the show began.

"The Man Who Saved the World" aka "Turkish Star Wars" was a truly awful movie. Arguably, it was the worst movie ever made. Everything about it, including the soundtrack, had been plagiarized from something. Alex leaned over and whispered, "Too bad Burnside didn't stay for the movie. He'da felt right at home." I stifled a laugh.

The plot involved a lot of skeletons and spaceships and such. The visuals were mostly pirated portions of *Star Wars* as well as newsclips from both the U.S. and Russia. The soundtrack included themes from *Raiders of the Lost Ark, Planet of the Apes*, and other films too numerous to mention. The audience, including many eminent astronomers, was raucous. Even Letitia produced a shrill whistle.

It was a great night.

I started the car and turned to Alex. "Are you thinking what I'm thinking?"

Alex nodded. "I am that."

We reached home exhausted.

Chapter 16

October 24, 1991

We picked up two bags of not-quite-rotten apples and another two bags of Certified Good ones, stowed them in the trunk, and motored to the Alpaca Toll Booth. The alpacas hurried to the fence as soon as we arrived, but this time the llamas edged them back a little. We threw the apples over the fence and the llamas moved aside to let the little critters get their treats. But the llamas stayed close. We were mystified.

Daryl walked up, accompanied by Claudia. Claudia grinned. "Now that Sam has cleared us all, what do you think?"

Alex grinned back. "I think we'd like to take you up on your offer."

Daryl wasn't grinning. "Before we shake on it, lemme show you something." He took us to a section of the fence about five yards away and pointed. A hole had been cut in the fence and then patched. "Someone tried to break in about two o'clock this morning. C'mon up to the house and we'll tell you about it."

We all got in the car and drove up.

"You can get that cuppa now," Claudia said.

The front door of the house opened directly onto the kitchen. It was spacious and modern. A table, looking like a smaller version of the refectory table at USAO, sat in the middle of the room. Six chairs that appeared to be Shaker-made ranged around it. The table was set for four, with pottery mugs and plates. The plates each held a piece of coffee cake. More coffee cake was in a basket. Claudia brought the coffeepot to the table and we sat.

"What happened," Daryl began, "was that we got woke up by a huge rumpus outside. We got up in time to see the llamas busting out of the paddock and chasing a guy toward the fence. I guess he made it to the hole because we didn't see any parts of him between there and the paddock. I patched the hole, told the llamas they were good boys, and we went back to bed.

"Now I don't know if that'll make any difference on you wanting the cabin."

"No." Alex and I in unison.

"Daryl," Alex said. "We live in the city. Break-ins happen all the time. I even got shot in front of my house."

"My word!" Claudia said.

"Do you know what the man was after?" I asked.

"Hard to tell," Daryl answered. "Whatever it was, the fella didn't want to come up the path and activate the house's security lights. Doesn't seem like he knew about the llamas. We figure he either wanted to rustle himself some alpacas – they're all valuable animals and we've got one champion that's worth a real bundle – or he wanted to steal something out of the cabin. We'll order security lights for the cabin later this morning."

"Wow," said Alex. "We were wondering why the llamas were being so protective of the herd."

"They'll do that, if they think there might be danger. We had a tree come down in a storm a year or so back and the llamas stuck close to the herd for almost a week," Claudia said.

"Well, if you're okay with that, I had a little agreement drawn up. It just says that you're responsible for what we talked about the other day – utilities and upkeep – and for anything you break. And we have to give each other three months notice if we want you to move or you want to move. That sound okay?"

"It does," I said.

Daryl walked over to the kitchen counter and picked up two copies of the agreement. "We've signed 'em already. You take 'em, look 'em over, and if they're good, sign both copies, keep one and drop the other one off on your way to work tomorrow.

"Oh, and by the way. We never put a lock on the cabin door, but if you want one, I'll have it done when the security lights get installed."

Alex and I looked at each other. Then we both shook our heads. With two four hundred pound llamas to protect us, who needs a lock?

"You know," I said to Alex as he maneuvered the curves, "Chuck may think we stayed in the cabin last night. You interrupted before I could tell him we weren't going to stay."

"Yeah."

We drove to LIT in silence. We weren't happy with our thoughts.

Ethel accosted me on the way to my office. "Well," she smirked, I guess I won't file a grievance after all."

"I'm relieved," I said.

"No," she continued smirkily, "I've just had a great offer from the private sector." She handed me an envelope. I opened it and read the contents. Her resignation was effective two weeks from this date, October 24, 1991. She would take those two weeks as vacation time.

I shook her hand. "Congratulations, I'm sure it will be a great opportunity for you. But we had best follow procedures. I'll call Lenore and she will stay with you while you pack your things."

"You mean now?"

"Yes. Once you've resigned, those are the official procedures."

I returned to my office and called Lenore. "Did you fire her?"

"No. She resigned."

"Hmmm," said Lenore. "I'll get to her office right now."

I called Alex and gave him the results of The Welsh Rabbit charade. "Hot damn!" he said. "I didn't know those were the procedures when someone resigned."

"They may not be. I just made them up."

"I am in awe," said my spouse. "Give me a half hour and I'll be at your place."

Lenore stopped in my office on the way back to her desk. "She has removed her things, said farewell to her colleagues, and has left."

I gave her the envelope. "Please get this processed as quickly as possible."

Lenore smiled. "I'll have it completed by the end of the day. I don't know how you did it, but you have my sincere congratulations. Shall I inform Dr. Pie?"

"Please. And Mr. Cromarty also, if you don't mind. They should hear it from you."

Gratified, Lenore went off to be the bearer of glad tidings.

Five minutes later my phone rang. Pie and Don. "How'd you do it?"

I gave them the story of the two sleazebags. "Geez," Don said, "I've heard stories about people pulling that scam but I never thought it would work."

"I don't think it would have worked if they had been government guys. But the private sector is woefully uninformed about the wily ways of the Feds. Best thing of all is that she's out of the system as soon as Lenore gets the papers pushed. She thinks she can do it today."

Pie entered the conversation. "If Lenore says it will be done today, you can bet it'll happen."

I waited for Alex and then we brought Don and Pie up to date over lunch in the cafeteria. We hadn't told them about the cabin, so we had to start from there.

"I can't think of any reason why Chuck would want to do me harm, particularly now when I'm about to recommend him for a job he wants."

Don said, "I can't either. I think we've still got the same four suspects."

Pie nodded. "But Bea, stay out of USAO until we get this solved. Don wants me to promote you to the vacant SES slot. I'd like you to be in one piece when it goes through."

"Hey! That's great. What's her title?" said my husband and cheering section.

Pie laughed. "We're going to split the duties. Don will be Director of Operations and Bea will be Director of Management. In other words, nothing will change."

"Can you get it through?" I asked.

"If we solve this, the Secretary will give me whatever I ask."

"But OPM?"

"They won't buck the Secretary."

We went back to our offices and worked until about 4:30, when Alex called. "It's a gorgeous day," he announced. "Let's take off and look at the leaves before it gets dark."

We drove slowly up the mountain, passing USAO, passing the Pumpkin Shoot, and then slowly down.

"How about stopping at Hamburgers And for an early dinner?" Alex asked.

"Absolutely."

By the time we finished eating, it was after 6:00 and the sun had set. Alex turned on the headlights and we started the drive back.

"I'll miss that place when we've finished with USAO," Alex

remarked. "It's too far from LIT to have lunch there."

"Too true. But we can probably find some excuse to drive there on weekends in the spring and fall. The cabin is closer to it than Alexandria is."

Alex pulled off the road and turned on the flashers. We had a very inventive snoggle undisturbed by Maryland law enforcement.

Eventually, we got back on the road. We drove up the mountain. Alex's warble was a loud, off-key rendition of "My Name is John Wellington Wells."

As we approached USAO, we noticed a light on in one of the offices. "That's Worley's," I said. "We should stop."

Alex agreed. We parked around the curve of the lot, next to Worley's car. I knocked on the office door. No response. I found my key and we walked in. Two items sat on his desk: one was a stamped, addressed envelope, the other a document with a "To whom it may concern" cover sheet.

I peered into the dome. Worley was sitting in the dim light on the chair next to the control box. "Wait here and keep an eye on us," I said. "I'll talk with Worley."

Alex nodded.

I opened the door to the dome and stepped out of the office.

"Hello, Worley."

Worley looked up. "Hello, Bea. It's all over, isn't it?"

"Yes, it is. Worley, did you kill your brother?"

Worley was shocked. "My God, no! I loved him. Bea. I'm not a monster. I'm just a bloke whose life got away from him. I'd like to tell you about it. Do you have time to listen?"

I nodded. "Of course." I looked around the dome. "Let me go back to your office and get a chair. I have the feeling this will be a long story."

"Too right."

I went to the office and got the desk chair. I turned out the light so that Alex could move closer without being seen, and went back to the dome, leaving the office door slightly ajar.

I sat down and Worley began his narrative.

"It all started when that girl accused me of raping her."

"Did you do it?"

"Oh, yes. I don't know what came over me. I never did anything like that before and haven't since. But I raped her all right. I got myself a lawyer and he told me not to worry. I should just get some friends of mine to say that they had all had sex with her, and the jury would just think she was a slut and dismiss the charges."

"And that was all it would take?"

"Yeh. I think so. This was Australia in the '70s. We weren't very enlightened then. For all I know, we still aren't. Anyway, the police were still investigating so I wasn't in jail yet. And I really didn't want to do what the lawyer said."

"Oh?"

"Well, you see I had pretty much done that girl a lot of damage already. And if I got her labeled a slut, that would ruin her life. Don't you think?"

"Yes, I do."

"So since I was still free, I called Worley – my brother, I'm Wally – and we decided to meet up in Alice Springs and walk in the outback. Whenever I got in trouble or didn't know what to do I always called Worl and we always walked in the outback. So there we were, with our backpacks and Worl says to me that it was hot and he'd like to rest a bit. We stopped and squatted and all of a sudden Worl gives a little yelp and just keels over. He was dead before I ever got to him." Wally stopped.

"I'm so sorry," I said.

"Yeh. Well, I cried for a bit. I didn't know what I'd do without Worley. He was always there for me. Anyway, I looked in his backpack and his wallet was there. It had his passport and his airline ticket and a letter from the States telling him where to go and who would meet him and giving him the details of his new employment. Worl and I looked a lot alike. He was only a little more than a year older than me. So I thought, 'Worley, you're here for me this one last time.' and I switched wallets with him. Then I loaded him on my back and hoofed it to Alice Springs. No one knew us there, so there were no problems. According to the official records, a doctor had certified that Walter Doolittle had died of a heart attack, only living relative was Worley Doolittle, who authorized cremation."

"And that was that?"

"That was certainly that. I used the airline ticket and took his job.

But I'm no astronomer, see. I belonged to an astronomy club, so I could talk the talk but I couldn't walk the walk. So I kept getting shunted around until I wound up here."

"All in all, not a bad landing place."

Worley gave a half smile. "Not bad at all. Except for that slimebag Call-me-Colonel and the grommet who's supposed to work for Chuck, I like 'em all. You never met that codger, Lazuli. He used to like me to come in his office and he'd tell me stuff about the old days in astronomy. I never said much to him – afraid he'd tell me to pull me head in. I miss the old bastard.

"I even got myself a hobby. If the Olympics had ever authorized a Pumpkin Shoot, I'da been in for the gold."

As Wally's narrative progressed, it became more and more Australian.

"Everything would have been sweet except while I was on the West Coast, I met this sheila and, well, you know. So when I got transferred here, we didn't know what to do. Neither of us had a brass razoo so we couldn't keep flying back and forth. Then one day I found this meeting in California. And man, I was on a lurk. Until that fire broke out in the banquet room kitchen. Wumpus caught me and I was up a gum tree."

"But surely that wasn't worth killing him for."

"Fair dinkum, if that was all there was to it. But if anyone really investigated, the whole thing might've come out. I came here on a false passport. I don't know if I'da been put in prison or deported back to Australia. If it was Australia, that rape thing would be there waiting for me. No, it woulda been hooroo, Wally."

"How did you ever manage to get Wumpus onto the Pumpkin Shoot field?"

Wally snorted. "Well, at the end of the day, the bloke calls me into his office and lets me know what's up. So I says to him, look you got this all wrong and I can explain it. But first I gotta do something. And he says, 'What's so important?'

"So I tell him that some of the guys from NASA are thinking about organizing a touch football game and they wanted a few of us to check out good places. I was supposed to check out the Pumpkin Shoot field, but I have to tell them tonight if it looks like a good place. They were gonna make the decision tonight. Why didn't Wumpus come with me and after we take a squizz, we can go get a beer, and I'll tell him the story. So he says okay.

"Now remember, the Pumpkin Shoot near here doesn't have those close-in targets like the one up the mountain. Just big targets about a football field away. When we get there, of course, it's dark and the place is closed. They don't lock up but they turn the flood lights on so people might be afraid to sneak in. I ask George if he's ever seen how the cannon works and he says no, but he'd like to. So I load a pumpkin and turn on the compressor and tell Wumpus to walk a little way down the field where he can get a good squizz but don't get near the big targets or he might get hit. When he gets where I want him I tell him to stop. He never saw it coming.

"I got the hell out of there – didn't even stop to turn off the compressor."

"My goodness!"

Another half-smile from Wally. "In the words of your Mae West, 'Goodness had nothing to do with it.'

"I thought that was the end of it. And then Pottle shows up. I was at the control box when in he walks. Now he hasn't seen Worl for some twenty years, but he recognized him – it was really me – right away. I gave him the big welcome and asked if he'd like to see the place and of course he said yes. I opened the slit and told him to meet me up on the catwalk. I'd go get some binoculars. So up he goes and I set the dome to go around. And that was it – again.

"All I had to do then was to corrupt the magnetic tape. Gomping cracking a fruity was a godsend – easy to blame it all on him."

I had nothing to say. Nothing at all.

"Pottle left his briefcase at the bottom of the stairs. I took a look inside. Old Lazuli's notes were in there and a journal. Nothing about me, so I turned it over to Krackov. It would be good if the notes saw the light of day.

"Then you started closing in. I started thinking about how I was going to finish you. I'm a little in love with you, you know."

"No, I didn't know."

"Well, doesn't matter now. Then I thought, Wally, you're not a monster but you're on your way to being one. Stop now."

"Will you come with me and surrender to the sheriff?'

"Absobloodylutely. But Bea, on my desk is a letter to my sheila. I wouldn't want the sheriff reading it. Would you mail it for me?

"Sure."

"And one more thing. I'd like to take a squizz at what I'll be leaving behind. I'll open the slit and go out on the catwalk one last time."

He opened the slit and walked up the stairs.

I went back to Alex in the office. Tears had streaked his face.

"He really isn't a monster," I said.

"No. Just a bloke whose life got away from him."

We held one another for a while. "He's not coming back down, is he?" Alex asked.

"No." I picked up the envelope, but not the document.

Alex said, "We don't have to tell anyone except Pie that we were here when he walked up the stairs.

"They'll want to know why we didn't try to stop him. That's not something I'd like to explain. Aside from us, it would cause problems at LIT and the Department. Let's wait half an hour and then call Sam. It will be impossible then for the cops to tell exactly when Doolittle jumped."

I concurred. "We saw Wally's car, came in, and found the slit open. We got alarmed."

"Good enough. Just remember to call him Worley."

Alex turned the light on and brought the chair back to Wally's office. We stood there holding hands for a while. Then we called Sam.

Afterword

Still October 1992

Lieutenant Colonel Burnside walked smartly into the building, as usual, on the stroke of 10:00. Shows the minions that he is not a slave to the 9:00am start time. As he marched toward his office he was intercepted by Lorrie. "Sir, there was a message for you. Colonel Bogle would like you to be in his office at noon – oops, I mean 12 pip emma."

"Do you have the message slip?"

"Of course, sir."

"Well done, Mrs. Loofus, please file it."

"Yes, sir." She turned away and stuck out her tongue.

Burnside walked to his office and shut the door. What could Bogle want? Of course! The Observatory was about to be transferred to civilian control. Bogle must want to personally convey Burnside's new assignment. And almost certainly give him advance notice of his promotion to full colonel. Of course. That was it. Burnside did a little jig. At long last he would receive the recognition he deserved.

He pressed the button on the loudspeaker. "Everyone," he said to the mini-multitude, "please meet immediately in the common room."

Burnside stood at the head of the table. "My dear colleagues," he intoned, "as you know, you will soon be under civilian control and I will have to leave you. I hope, as you transition into civilian life, you will remember and continue to practice the discipline I have fostered while you were in my care. I will be moving on to another post and, I may tell you in confidence, a significant promotion. I will leave you now. Please have my belongings packed and sent to my current home address. I have enjoyed our association. I bid you farewell."

And with that, he executed a smart salute and left.

The audience sat stunned, searching for adequate words.

Dr. Krakov found them. "Mommy may fwow up."

Lieutenant Colonel Burnside walked into Colonel Bogle's Pentagon office and executed yet another smart salute. "Good morning, Sir. I would like to say that I am honored to be here."

Bogle was standing behind a comfortably messy desk. He was a pleasant looking man, gray hair, ruddy complexion, just the hint of a very unmilitary paunch and with an underlying manner that said it would be unwise to mess with him.

"Is that right? Well, before you get overwhelmed by the honor, Lieutenant Colonel, please examine the documents on that table over there." He pointed his chin at the table.

Bogle watched with some satisfaction as Burnside was confronted with a Burnside-attributed article in the *Astronomical Journal* alongside a facsimile of Morgan Lazuli's notes.

"You have the right," said Colonel Bogle, "to remain silent...."

Epilogue

DoTI offered the Astronomer position to Dr. Randolph Smathers who, on Bad Movie Night, had wistfully remarked that he would enjoy looking at asteroids. The position was advertised and Dr. Smathers won in a walk. He loves his new job. The Secretary's twelve-year-old kid comes by every chance he gets. Dr. Smathers is his tutor. Tutoring the kid has opened a new extracurricular career for Dr. Smathers. He has gone on the High School lecture circuit, mentors bright students as they prepare for their science fairs, and is, in other words, having a ball.

Chuck Hadaman has also struck it rich. His job as LIT's facilities manager suits him wonderfully. He spends his days doing what he loves to do and has access to resources able to do what he hates to do – namely, paperwork. There were a few grumbles when he was given the position, but they faded away shortly. His view of management is that a large part of a manager's job is to make it easier for the staff to do their jobs. That, plus the fact that he's such a nice guy quelled the grumbles. He also came out of the closet. No one gave a hoot.

Bobby got a great offer from MIT, and after a little arm-twisting by Pie, they agreed to allow Bobby to continue to work with Letitia on Lazuli's notes, with the proviso that Bobby visit MIT to give a bi-monthly lecture on the current results of his work. Bobby did not find this a hardship.

Lorrie, to her delight, was pregnant. She and her husband bought a little house near the University of Maryland. Alex, Bea, Letitia, Bobby, and Chuck were invited to the combined baby shower and house warming. They all came bearing gifts. Alex and Bea brought Rocky, an Alpaca Teddy Bear. This necessitated a trip to FAO Schwarz in New York, a journey that convinced them that New York was a nice place to visit but.... Bobby brought a custom-bound book of his limericks. Chuck fabricated a metal model of the Morgan Lazuli Observatory (formerly known as USAO). Letitia's contribution was a beautifully crafted kaleidoscope that tumbled the stars and planets. Lorrie's astrophysicist husband immediately confiscated it and declared it his own.

Things did not work out so well for Ethel. She did not survive her probationary period at the law firm of Sleazebag & Sleazebag. She was fired within a month. She called Bea and demanded her old job back. Bea explained that her resignation had already gone through the required procedures and she was out of the Federal system. She was welcome to answer announcements for jobs open to the public. LIT would not advertise for her replacement. She was, Bea told her, irreplaceable.

As for Ambrose Burnside, the Army took care of him.

No one knows what happened to Tristram Gomping.

Alex and Bea love their little cabin and their landlords. Sheriff Sam, Deputy Joe, and Buddy the grocer visit on occasional weekends. Every once in a while they, plus the Cokers, Alex, and Bea grace The Rabbit Hole with their presence.

God is in Heaven. All's right with the World.

GLOSSARY OF YIDDISH WORDS AND PHRASES USED IN THIS BOOK

Bubele — darling, sweetie, a term of affection

Gantseh Macher — a big shot

Genug — enough, sufficient

Gevalt — uh oh, an expression of dismay

Gonif — thief

Macher — an important person, but not as important as a Gantseh Macher

Maven — an expert in a given field

Mazel Tov — congratulatons

Mentsh — a person of integrity, a good guy

Meshuggina — a nutcake, a crazy person

Mishegas — craziness

Nosh - a snack

Nu — an all purpose word that can mean anything from "how are you doing" to "tell me". The English equivalent is "So?"

Oy — a disapproving sigh

Seykhel — smarts, common sense

Shlep — drag, lug

Shmegegge — a pain in the butt, a fool

Shtunk — a really bad guy

Tsuris — serious trouble

Tuches — backside, rear end

Vey ist mir —woe is me

GLOSSARY OF AUSTRALIAN SLANG USED IN THIS BOOK

Bloke — man, guy
Brass Razoo — a non-existent coin of trivial value
Codger — an eccentric old man
Crack a Fruity — go crazy
Fair Dinkum — true, genuine
Grommet — an idiot
Holy Dooly — an exclamation of surprise
Hooroo — good bye
I'll Be Stuffed — an expression of surprise
Old bastard — term of affection among male friends
On a Lurk — on to a good thing
Pull Your Head In — shut up, you don't know what you're taling about
Sheila — a woman
Slime — an untrustworthy brown nose
Squizz — look
Stone the crows — another expression of surprise
Up a gum tree — in trouble

Made in the USA
Charleston, SC
22 June 2013